By Vanessa Mulberry

The First Act

Published by Dreamspinner Press
www.dreamspinnerpress.com

VANESSA MULBERRY

THE

FIRST
ACT

DREAMSPINNER
PRESS

Published by

DREAMSPINNER PRESS

5032 Capital Circle SW, Suite 2, PMB# 279, Tallahassee, FL 32305-7886 USA
www.dreamspinnerpress.com

The First Act
© 2016 Vanessa Mulberry.

Cover Art
© 2016 AngstyG.
www.angstyg.com
Cover content is for illustrative purposes only and any person depicted on the cover is a model.

ISBN: 978-1-63477-781-0
Digital ISBN: 978-1-63477-782-7
Library of Congress Control Number: 2016913747
Published October 2016
v. 1.0

Printed in the United States of America
(∞)
This paper meets the requirements of
ANSI/NISO Z39.48-1992 (Permanence of Paper).

For my readers

With thanks to Desi, Jo, Victoria, and Sue,
who have all saved me from untold embarrassment.

CHAPTER ONE

April 1594

AFTER THREE long months filled with hopes, dreams, and more than the occasional sinful fantasy, at last the day arrived. The celebrated playing company, Goldfox's Men, returned to Oxford, and William Moodie hurried through the city's bustling streets to see them. It would be the tenth time he watched them perform, and he was as eager as ever.

The players had been touring for seventeen months, driven out of their home in London by the plague. William had been to every Oxford performance since, proudly telling everyone he met that Geoffrey Moodie, one of the company's leading men, was his cousin. Few were impressed. Geoffrey had his admirers, but he wasn't the draw, not even for William. The crowds came to see one man—Richard Brasyer.

William whistled happily to himself as he went, too wrapped up in his thoughts to care what was happening around him. In his mind he was already in front of the stage, watching Richard perform. Perhaps today their eyes would meet, and William might communicate the secrets in his heart. He often gave himself over to dreams of their union, though he knew such fantastical thoughts had no place in reality, but just the idea of being in the actor's presence again was a thrill. William's whole body tingled, stomach aflutter, and he wasn't even at the theater yet.

Ah, Richard Brasyer. Handsome, wonderful, perfect Richard Brasyer.

Richard's looks were well favored, and he wore no paint to accentuate them. He had eyes as green as oak leaves in June, a perfectly straight nose, and a tidy beard, which was as dark as the thick black waves of hair on his head. Last time Richard visited Oxford, his hair was falling around his ears, which was long by both his own standards and the current fashion, but William didn't care if Richard's hair grew down to his knees. He would still be in love with him.

Arriving at the inn where the company would be performing, William met Geoffrey at the door, and they embraced. His cousin was still chubby, despite the company's straitened circumstances, and his blond hair was beginning to gray. He was forty years old—twice William's age—and he looked it.

"Cousin William!" Geoffrey said merrily, before looking around him for the rest of their family. His face fell when he saw they had not come. "Am I out of favor?"

William grinned at him. "Never. Your sister Jane is in her childbed, so they remain in the village. I volunteered to come and give you the news."

Geoffrey smiled, but it was a tight-lipped, nervous thing. William understood. They'd already buried two of Geoffrey's sisters.

"How is she faring?"

"Well. The babe is here, and it's a boy. He was feeding when I left."

Geoffrey clapped his hands together and turned his face to the heavens. "What tidings! And such good timing. The plague is leaving London, and we are on our way back to Southwark. There will be no performances until we are set up next week at the theater, so I'm sure I will be able to stay a few days."

This was supposed to be good news, so William smiled, but he took no pleasure from it. If the company returned to the theaters of London, they would not drag themselves out to Oxford. William would likely never see Richard Brasyer again.

Geoffrey led him to the courtyard for the performance and left him in a position where he would be at the front of the crowd. It was early spring, and the temperature was mild, with little breeze and blue skies. Clement weather always brought in more heads, but William was continually surprised by the number of people like himself who braved the rain and cold for a chance of entertainment.

He leaned on a post, knowing he would be standing for a long time, and listened to other patrons talk of Irish rebellions and Catholic plots. He could understand their fascination. Conspiracy was not a part of his life on the farm; it was another world, filled with mystery and excitement beyond anything he would ever know. But the thought of adventure did not move him now. He could barely take in a word of what they said.

William did keep an ear open for the womenfolk in the crowd, who whispered to each other how well they regarded Richard. That was more to his interest. He teased a few of the girls while they awaited the start of the show, pretended to humor them when they giggled over Richard, and buried his sadness at the company's departure before it buried him.

The crowd's chatter lulled as a beating drum signaled the play was to begin. William, determined to enjoy his last moments in Richard's presence, reminded himself that the love of his life didn't know who he was. Even with Geoffrey as their mutual acquaintance, they'd never met. What did it matter if William never saw him again?

My whole world. That's what matters.

Geoffrey carefully kept his colleagues away from his family, but he couldn't keep the family away from the shows. That was how William fell in love with a man he had never been introduced to. He had fancied Richard from the first time he saw him step out onto the stage, but when Richard tenderly kissed a young male actor dressed up like a maiden, William wanted him more desperately than he wanted any other man before. His lips ached to be kissed like that.

Seventeen months hence—William had been counting—and he hadn't got that kiss. He didn't even know how to go about getting such a thing, but he expected Richard would be kissing that boy again this afternoon.

Lucky bastard.

The performance seemed to race by, though William's stiff legs felt the passage of time. He watched Richard wrap himself in intrigue and swordfight his way across the stage with the conviction of a man who did such things every day. He was incredible. When it was over, William hung back as the rest of the audience left, waiting for Geoffrey to approach and hoping he might get one last glimpse of Richard Brasyer.

His cousin ambled over a short while later, still grinning. "What did you think?"

"As good as ever," William assured him.

"That bad, eh? Well, no matter. I will still be paid. Now, you must hurry back to the village and make ready for our arrival."

William was sure his heart stopped. "Our?" he asked, careful not to appear too excited.

"When I gave the others my news, they offered to stop at the village tonight and put on a brief show. We'll bring meat and mead enough for all, but we'll need light to perform by and a place to sleep. Half a dozen pallets in the hay barn will do. We can do three to a bed if you all can."

That meant eighteen men. They were all coming.

Richard was coming.

WILLIAM RACED back to the village. Mother and baby were still healthy and happy, everyone was in good cheer, and news of a free feast and a play only improved the mood. By dusk, most had lined up on the common awaiting their visitors.

Standing in the middle of the row, after his older brothers and male cousins but before the girls and the children, William waited. Geoffrey went first down the line, but the rest of the players appeared to be in no order of importance. Six men passed before William found Richard standing in front of him, shaking his hand.

Richard was even better-looking up close. His skin was unblemished, but he had a few lines around his eyes that betrayed his experience, and even a few gray hairs on his head and in his beard. He wore a dark gray doublet trimmed with vibrant blue taffeta, matching slops, and both a sword and a dagger hung from his belt. He cut quite a figure.

"Hollo," he greeted William warmly, "I'm Richard."

The moment was much longed for, and William had rehearsed it a hundred times in his head, but now his mind was blank.

"H-H-Hollo," he stammered, feeling his face flush. It was a stark contrast to the chill that ran through his body as gooseflesh pimpled his skin.

Richard smiled at him indulgently and then moved on to greet the rest of the family.

William found himself shaking hands with another member of the company, and his one chance to impress Richard was gone.

With the light fading, the actors set up quickly for the performance and were soon in the middle of one of the shorter plays in their repertoire. William sat on the grass with his brothers and watched, but he struggled to enjoy the play after making such a fool of himself in front of Richard.

This was the price of his idolatry, and he hated it. If only he loved Richard less… but how could he? Richard was perfect.

When the play was over, the eating and drinking began. Everyone crowded around the fires and drank to the health of the new mother and her child, who were both resting abed.

William took a stool and sat back in the dark to watch the merry group. He had already made a fool of himself, and he didn't want to do anything worse. Besides, Richard was telling stories for the children, and William had the best position from which to look upon him unheeded.

Richard's face was illuminated by firelight, and if he felt William's intense gaze, it did not worry him. Here was a man used to being watched. A quick glance at the villagers' rapt faces confirmed William wasn't the only person who couldn't drag his eyes away from the mesmerizing actor.

"There you are! I could barely see you hiding in the dark."

William looked away from Richard for a second to see his eldest brother, Francis, approach, carrying a stool and a jug of mead. Francis seemed a little drunk and was in high spirits.

"Shh! I'm enjoying the story, and you will ruin it," William chided in a low voice, hoping Francis would take the hint and go away. He didn't want to miss a moment.

"He's good, isn't he?"

"He's the best," William said, careful not to sigh.

His brother wasn't fooled. "I noticed you forgot how to use your tongue when he spoke to you."

Everyone must have seen it, but William only cared about Richard's opinion. He didn't think it would be good. "I hope he comes back. I'll do better next time."

"You are in thrall. But I don't think you want to be like him."

So that's what Francis thought. William knew he should be relieved, but he would have liked to reveal his passion to someone, anyone. It wasn't an easy secret to keep. "Why wouldn't I want to be like him?" he demanded, insulted on Richard's behalf. "He's marvelous. Every season he's better than the last."

"I'll grant you he's talented."

"And handsome."

Francis snorted and leaned closer as he whispered, "The womenfolk love him, but I think he looked too comfortable kissing that pretty red-haired boy in the play. He's the talk of London when he's there, and that's what they're all saying."

William whipped his head around and attempted to search his brother's face in the dark.

"Where did you hear that gossip? You've never been farther than ten miles from the village, let alone to London. How could you know who he has in his bed?"

"I heard it from our cousin," Francis replied with a chuckle. "So don't feel bad about embarrassing yourself in front of him. You may have done yourself a favor."

Francis let him be, and William continued to watch Richard alone, fearing his stuttering nerves had cost him even more dearly than he first imagined. He barely noticed when Richard bade the crowd good night and left with his apprentice, the youth he kissed every time he took to the stage. Only when they were completely consumed by the dark did William realize what was happening.

Thankfully he knew where they were going, and he could get there first. The pallets had been set up in the barn as Geoffrey requested, and they would be alone in there this early. William had an idea of what they would do—his education on such matters being a particularly toe-curling church sermon and Francis's bragging about what he did with his lady. William stirred at the thought of two men together.

Silently he slipped away from the gathering and headed toward the barn, hurrying around and ahead of them. He could hear the two performers walking behind him and noted the lad was happy-drunk, while Richard seemed sober enough.

They came to a halt at the barn door. William stopped abruptly alongside one of its walls, hoping they couldn't see or hear him. After a moment's silence, Richard grumbled, "Step back, Nick. Your breath smells like cunny."

"We're not getting paid to be here. I decided I might as well enjoy myself," Nick replied with a drunken chuckle.

"There are herbs in my bag to freshen your breath."

"I better rub them on my cock too if the smell bothers you."

"Delightful."

"What? You should try it one day. You might find you like the taste."

"I tasted it in my youth, and it didn't please my palate."

They entered the barn. William circled around to a shuttered window, jumping back against the wall as it was pushed open from the inside to let in some starlight. He did not risk trying to look through it.

"How did I ever end up with a dedicated woman-lover in my bed?" Richard asked wearily.

"Men might not be for me, but money's another matter." Nick mumbled the reply through a mouthful of mint, and a faint waft of its scent made its way out to William. He realized then that they were only steps away, and he pressed back against the wall, afraid of being caught. Suddenly Nick poked his head out of the window and spat out his mint leaves. He returned a few moments later and did the same with a mouthful of water.

Straw rustled as one or both of them lay down on a pallet.

"So do you want me for bed work or not?" Nick asked. "I'll give you a suck if you fancy it."

"I did a few minutes ago, but I'm not so keen now."

"You've got me feeling guilty."

Richard laughed. "Don't feel guilty about what you are. You don't like men. I don't like women. Other people like both and some like neither. The world is big enough for all of us, even if the law says otherwise."

This is an education!

They were silent a moment, and then Nick asked, "Does this mean I'm getting my wages cut?"

They both giggled.

"Why not play a part for me tonight?" Richard suggested. "I've no room in my bed for a cynic like you, but a charming country boy would please me."

"H-H-Hollo," Nick said in a perfect imitation of William's stammer.

"Yes, he's the one."

William clasped his hand over his mouth to stop himself from gasping. He wasn't sure whether he should feel shame or excitement. Both feelings were quickly replaced by arousal as the pallet rustled again. Two soft thuds followed as a pair of boots hit the floor, and

William imagined Richard removing his hose. More rustling, of both straw and blankets, and finally they were still.

William's cock ached to be touched as he listened and pictured what he could not see. There was no slap of flesh, and Richard was moaning softly. Nick must be using his mouth, but William couldn't decide if he was lying on the pallet or was on his knees. However he worked, he sounded very good at his job.

Suddenly Richard said, "You should be clumsier. You do that better than my country boy would."

"You can pay him to come do it if that's what you want."

William's heart thumped wildly in his chest. Should he interrupt them? It didn't sound like Richard would mind.

Then Richard disappointed him. "All I want is for you to do your work with a little less skill and a lot more thought."

"And what will be your thoughts?"

With a hum of pleasure that told William Nick had returned to his work, Richard murmured, "Simpler pleasures."

William remained until muffled moans told him Richard came off. He dashed away from the barn and out into the woods, where he hoped he would be undisturbed. There he slumped against a tree and took himself in hand. It didn't take much for him to find release.

After a quick cleanup with some leaves, William returned to his parents' home and got into bed. He could not sleep. All night long, he dreamed of Richard, turning over in his mind what he'd heard. Tonight had been his only chance, and he'd let Richard slip away into the night with someone who clearly didn't appreciate him. Not that Richard seemed to appreciate Nick much either. Their relationship was definitely one of convenience, not love.

In the morning, William woke to find the barn empty, save for the pallets. The company had moved on, only the embers of the fires on the common left to remind him they were ever there. He surveyed the scene glumly from the barn door.

Then a figure came into view, and he remembered one connection he still held to Richard. He couldn't let it go.

"They've gone," Geoffrey called as he ambled across the grass. "It's a long road to London. Best to set off early."

William moved aside as Geoffrey entered the barn and inspected it to make sure nothing had been left behind.

"Help me shift these pallets, lad."

William obliged, grateful for the opportunity to talk with Geoffrey in privacy. "How long will you stay?" he asked casually, though his whole future depended on it.

"Only until Thursday morning."

That gave William two days to prepare himself and his family for his departure. They had been concerned when Geoffrey had gone off with an acting company but his success made them proud of him. William anticipated a far easier time than Geoffrey had experienced.

"When is your next performance?"

"Monday, assuming Richard has managed to get us into our usual theater by then. Another company might have their eyes on it."

"Does Richard often get what he wants?"

Geoffrey shot him a playful look and winked. "Not if I can help it."

William didn't for one minute think Richard and Geoffrey had ever been in competition for anything. He knew his cousin better than that. He rolled up a pallet and rested it against the wall, then went back for another. "I hear you've been telling Francis tales of London."

Geoffrey picked up another of the makeshift beds and carried it outside. "What of it? They're more interesting than what I've seen or done in the provincial towns we've been touring this past year."

"I don't doubt that. Why have you never told them to me?"

Geoffrey let out an embarrassed laugh but gave him a sympathetic smile when it was clear he was wounded. "When you're older, perhaps. Some things are not meant for young men's ears."

"I'm twenty!"

"And still living like a boy here in the house of my aunt and uncle. You're not ready to hear saucy tales. You toy with the girls like a master, but Francis tells me you've never seen it through."

William hadn't, and he was glad of his innocence for once. "That is precisely why you should take me with you when you return to town. It's time I got out into the world."

Geoffrey frowned, and William tried not to look too gleeful. His cousin had stumbled right into that.

"What has brought this on? Aren't you happy at home?"

"I am not unhappy, just mindful that this will not last forever. I am the youngest son, and it would be imprudent to not consider my future. There's nothing for me here. I could make a living for myself in London."

Raising an eyebrow, Geoffrey replied, "Or you could get yourself killed. London is not meant for gentle sorts like you. You can't cross the bridge without seeing thirty heads on pikes, and if someone wants your purse, they're as likely to cut you as the strings. It is dangerous, fetid, and diseased. You would not last a day, and your parents would never forgive me."

William noted that he hadn't said no. "I'll be fine," he said cheerfully. "And besides, you'll look after me."

"You'll not be my ward."

"Not for long."

"Not for a day. What do you intend to do when you get there?"

Get on the stage and kiss Richard Brasyer, of course.

"You've seen me act in plays on feast days," William reminded his cousin. "I seem to remember you saying I was quite good. I could join your band as a player."

Geoffrey laughed again, but no sympathy followed this time. "You don't have the ballocks for the stage, and even if you did, we don't need another man."

William remembered his stammering hollo to Richard yesterday. He had been nervous, but it cost him so dearly that he wouldn't allow shyness to get the better of him again. Besides, having heard Richard the night before, he possessed all the confidence he needed—he had attracted Richard with that stuttering hollo. He could do anything.

"I can do more than you imagine for now, and a position will come up. Until then I can do any other jobs you have."

"Such as?"

That, William hadn't considered, but he would empty the theater piss pots if it meant getting to London. "I can stitch a costume or sweep the floor if that's what you need."

"Women's work," Geoffrey muttered dismissively, but William had an inkling that the players did it themselves.

"I am not too proud for any job within your company. Please take me with you and let me prove myself."

"You'll hate it."

William noted again that he was yet to say the word *no*. "I won't," he promised. "I want to be an actor."

"It is harder work than it looks, and you're too old to apprentice. You should have asked me five years ago."

"I can learn as well now as I would have done back then. And I don't mind the low wage. It will be more than I have here."

"It will cost you more to live too."

William didn't expect riches, but he would need room and board, and a little for essentials. "You keep your apprentice," he said, believing that to be the norm.

"He costs me enough, and I don't need another."

Apprenticing with his cousin was the last thing William wanted. "What about Richard?" He asked the question as if working for the other lead had just occurred to him.

"I feared that was where this was going." Geoffrey let out a sigh. His eyes darted about to make sure they were alone; then he shuffled William into the barn and shut the door behind them. Tone hushed, he said, "Forget about Richard. You're not the first man who's had his head turned by him, and you won't be the last. He has a boy who serves him well, and you won't see him again. Aren't there girls enough in Oxford to catch your eye?"

William ignored that question. "All I want is to go to London and find work with your company. If I must wait for the position I want to become available, then I will."

"Please, William, don't ask me to do this. He will sully you."

"That is my goal."

"Then I am definitely not taking you."

Geoffrey snatched up the last two pallets from the corner and quickly headed for the barn door. He yanked it open violently and let it clatter against the wooden wall as he marched straight toward the house.

"Please, Geoffrey!" William begged, catching him and pulling him to a halt. "I am the youngest of four brothers. What is there for me here? Francis will get the land when my parents die, and I will have a pittance. The others have been bought apprenticeships, but there is no money for me to have one. I have no skills besides farming, no money for a tenancy. Have you forgotten your position was once the same? You have become a prosperous man in your profession. Do not deny me a good livelihood because Richard Brasyer has a taste for men."

"I do not care what he likes," Geoffrey hissed. "He is my friend and will do what he wants with my blessing. But you are my cousin and the youngest, at that. What would your mother say to me if she knew?"

"She would thank you for giving her youngest a chance in a family business. She will be made proud by my success, and my brothers will be envious. My father will thank you for allaying his fears for my future."

"They will not thank me. This is not a reputable business."

"It is not a bad one these days either, and you are much celebrated for your achievements. They've felt the weight of your moneybag. You think they wouldn't want that for me?"

Geoffrey dropped the pallets and rubbed his temples. William could see he'd hit his mark and his cousin had little fight left.

Pursing his lips, Geoffrey rallied for one last attempt at dissuading him. "If they weigh my coin now, they won't find it so heavy. It's feast or famine in this business, and times are tough. Besides, it's not the acting that will make you rich. You need a share in the company, and you cannot afford to buy one."

William would worry about that later. "You had your inheritance. One day I will have mine, albeit a small one. I can save, supplement it however I must, until I have the money. Let me find out what the business is like now before I sink what little cash I have into it. If I hate it, I may return home, and I've lost nothing. Isn't that better than me losing the lot later when I have the funds and you cannot stop me?"

His cousin shook his head slowly, but William could see he'd won him over.

"I'll give you the season," Geoffrey relented. "You will do any job I ask and get only one shilling a week. I will provide room and board, which is the same terms as my apprentice gets. If a position becomes available with one of the other sharers, no matter who it is, you will take it."

A familiar excitement grew in William's belly. It came and went with the playing company, but now he thought he would feel that way forever. "Thank you!" He hugged Geoffrey tightly. "You will not regret this, I swear it."

From the look of Geoffrey's face, he already was. William didn't mind. He was a week away from seeing Richard Brasyer again, and next time they met, he wouldn't stammer.

CHAPTER TWO

RICHARD SAT on the edge of the stage, surveying the sturdy wooden beams of the theater. It was not twenty years old but already felt ancient to him.

Humans had told stories since God created the Earth, and Richard considered himself part of that long and noble tradition. Even the plays were timeless, rewritten yesterday, but telling stories of events sometimes thousands of years in the past. People would probably still be performing them thousands of years into the future. There was a strange comfort in that.

He was in a fine mood and pleased to be back in his old home for two reasons. First, he made ten times the money, and second, the return to London meant old friends, new plays, and a real bed in his own room every night, which was more than was guaranteed on tour.

London hadn't changed much. Richard arrived to find Marlowe dead—an occupational hazard for any man who involved himself in intrigue as much as Kit did, even though Richard had always thought him particularly skilled at it—and the Upstart, Shakespeare, back with some new plays. If they were half as popular as his Henrys, Richard would have stiff competition, particularly if Burbage was around to lead.

None of that worried him right then. Anything was better than trawling the provinces.

The rest of the company arrived for the afternoon performance in twos and threes. Watching them file in, Richard could see the mood was high and there was an atmosphere of anticipation among them all. It would be their most generous pay in more than a year, and they were eager for it.

Geoffrey shuffled in last with his head down, shoulders bunched up around his ears. Richard's mind traveled back to the birth he'd helped to celebrate the previous week, and he hoped mother and child were well.

The two actors had been friends a long time, although they were little alike. Geoffrey didn't seem to mind Richard's male lovers, and

Richard didn't care that his friend sired bastards all over town. As the two biggest sharers in the company—owning 70 percent between them—they had a lot invested in their friendship, but Richard would have felt no different if they hadn't a penny to their names. Given their trade, one day they might not.

Jumping from the stage and into the pit, Richard went to greet him. "Friend!" he said, embracing Geoffrey warmly. "Is your sister well?"

"She was in good health when I left," Geoffrey replied with the forced cheer he normally reserved for the stage, patting Richard's back and shifting away awkwardly.

"And the babe?"

"He's a healthy boy."

"So tell me, why do you look so tense?"

Before Geoffrey could deny it, a young man stepped up beside them. Richard knew him instantly as a Moodie. He could not forget a face like that.

The lad was exquisitely handsome, with rich, brown, wavy hair that fell to his shoulders, and eyes so dark that, even at a short distance, Richard couldn't make out where the inky black ended and the iris ought to begin. His hair was scraped back now, and he didn't appear as nervous as he had previously, but he was unmistakably the youth who'd caught Richard's eye in the Oxfordshire countryside.

Richard had occupied himself with fantasies of his country boy several times since greeting him—usually first thing in the morning and last thing at night. What was he doing in London?

"Who's this?" he asked, smirking at the young man and wondering if Nick watched.

"My cousin, William."

"Cousin? Did we meet last week?"

He expected William to stammer again, but the lad replied confidently. "We weren't properly introduced, but I think you noticed me."

Richard's grin widened. He had not expected that or the seductive smile that followed it. "So what brings you to London?"

"I'm here to work."

"At what?"

"Whatever you wish."

Richard had not expected that either. "Geoffrey has employed you?" he asked, giving Geoffrey a sideways glance.

"Yes, but I hope to work for you one day. I am an admirer of yours."

"I am not short of those, and they don't usually ask a wage for the privilege. May we speak, Geoffrey?"

From the corner of his eye, Richard could see William looked troubled, but he ignored it as he and Geoffrey stepped away to talk.

When they were far enough apart that William would not hear their low voices, he said, "Do we no longer make the decision to take on men together? I have several cousins I should like to keep via the company coffers."

"I will cover his wage from my share until an apprentice's position becomes available. There's little for him in the village, and he's the youngest son. We could give him a chance."

Richard knew all too well the difficulty of being the youngest child. He felt a grudging sympathy for William in that respect. "What do you expect him to do until then?" he asked wearily.

"He'll do anything. He can work the door this afternoon."

"Can we trust him?"

"He's not got the wit to steal anything yet. Besides, he's in awe of you, and he wants to be an actor. He wouldn't risk his chance."

The last was said with a tinge of worry. Richard searched his friend's face. Geoffrey was unenthusiastic about the young man's presence, but he wasn't a man prone to optimism. He'd bothered to bring William, so the lad couldn't be entirely useless.

"All right," Richard relented. "Set him on the groundlings' door, but if he disappears with the money, you will be paying us all."

"I can't afford that!"

"Then you better hope he is as honest as you say."

William didn't look like a thief, but Richard thought him an easy target for one. He sat on the edge of the stage and watched William listen and nod attentively as Geoffrey explained what to do and how to avoid cutpurses. William looked across at Richard and smiled shyly when their eyes met. It would be interesting to see how far his admiration went.

"Why did you bring him?" Richard asked when Geoffrey finally joined him.

"He begged me, and he knew all the right things to say. He needs a chance. I am in a position to give him one."

"But you don't want him here?"

Geoffrey hesitated. He was holding something back, but Richard could not fathom what.

"He has as much opportunity to ruin himself as to improve his lot," Geoffrey eventually replied.

Richard would have guessed by his looks and manner that William was sensible enough, but he knew better than to judge a man on something as superficial as that. "He doesn't seem like the type."

"I would have said the same a week ago, but I think he's more determined of that than anything else."

"And yet you put him in charge of the money?"

"There's more than one way to ruin a man. You know that."

Dice, wine, women, men… yes, there were plenty of ways to do that, and those methods were for the fainter hearted. The Tower beckoned many a man who thought himself beyond such things. Whatever William's particular vice, Richard decided not to worry about it. The company already had its fair share of rogues. What was one more?

AFTER THE performance, the men all sat on the stage and eagerly awaited their pay.

William had been given the takings for all three doors and was counting it up in silence with a look of wonder on his face, chuckling to himself as he worked. That only increased the excitement among the others. Richard enjoyed their happiness, and even Geoffrey smiled.

When William was done, he cackled with childish glee. It must have been more money than he'd ever held in his life.

"Well, William," Richard pressed, "how much did we take?"

William handed the bag of coins over to Geoffrey. "Nine pounds, ten shillings, and sixpence," he said, laughing. "A king's ransom!"

The hired men and apprentices whooped and danced, certain they would get their wages and a promised bonus. The company hadn't taken above eighteen shillings—less than one pound—at a performance since they fled the capital, and this was something to celebrate. The sharers didn't look so happy.

"Are you sure?" Richard asked, glancing to Geoffrey, who was shaking his head and spitting blasphemies under his breath.

"I swear it," William squealed. "It's a fortune!"

Richard stepped up next to him and murmured, "Where's the rest? We normally take ten pounds in London, an angel more than that, and the theater was particularly crowded today."

"You do?" William's mirth was gone, replaced first by confusion, then panic.

Richard would wager his share that William hadn't taken the money, and a cutpurse would have had the lot. It must be one of their men recognizing an opportunity to blame it on the new boy. There was only one way to find out; he had to play along.

"Don't give me that wide-eyed innocence!" he roared.

William shrank back in fear. Although they were practically strangers, Richard did not like to see it.

In an instant, the men fell silent, with only Geoffrey's cursing filling the void. William looked to his cousin for help, but Richard knew he would get nothing from that quarter until his innocence was proven.

"I haven't had a farthing of it," William argued.

"Think carefully, boy, because in London, men are hanged for less. Your village cousins might have forgiven such a transgression with reparation and an apology, but the city is not so kind. You've picked a dangerous place to begin your career as a thief."

"I wasn't the only man on the door. This is all I was given. I swear it on your life. I-I-I mean, my life."

Ah, the nerves are still there, albeit buried deep.

"Prove it," Richard challenged. "Take your clothes off."

"What? No!"

"Let me search you. If there is money on you, I'll find it."

William blushed rosy red as he stripped. Soon he stood in only his shirt, which he pulled down at the front to cover his cock and balls. It was unseasonably warm for mid-April, and Richard gave William's muscular white thighs a leisurely gaze, not worried William would become cold.

He tossed the lad's clothes and shoes to Geoffrey, who searched them and found nothing, exactly as Richard had suspected.

Richard frowned at William as if confused and continued his search. He smoothed the young man's shirt down, finding only the hard lines of his chest and stomach hiding beneath it and two perky nipples poking the cloth. His eyes dipped lower, but he could see William was not excited by the touch.

It must be colder than I thought.

"Well, it's not you, unless there's a purse up your arse, but it looks too tight for that."

The others laughed. William's face turned a more vivid shade of scarlet.

Richard took William's clothes from Geoffrey and handed them back. "Sorry for the performance," he whispered softly to William. "I undressed you to confirm your innocence to the men. I think your blushes have proven that."

He turned his attention to the rest. "Let's find out who did take it."

One by one the others emptied out their pockets and allowed themselves to be searched until only Nick remained. Richard left him until last, hoping he was not the culprit. He trusted Nick more than the others because he knew him best. Perhaps that should have been reason enough to trust him least, but although he didn't think Nick was above thieving, Richard hadn't believed he would ever be the victim.

"You're not going to search me, are you?" Nick asked with an uneasy laugh. "You've seen me naked plenty of times."

"Give me your purse."

Nick swallowed nervously, tongue poking out to moisten his lips for the lie. "It's heavy today. I've been saving my wages."

He handed it over, and Richard felt the substantial weight. There was the stolen angel and more besides.

"Pay the men, Geoffrey," Richard said. "See the sharers right too, as if we'd had an angel more. Everyone can go for the day."

He waited silently while they collected their money and headed off to squander it in the taverns. When only Geoffrey, William, and Nick remained, it was time to hold his apprentice to account.

"Apologize to William," Richard began. "You could have cost him his future."

Nick scowled at the newcomer. "Sorry," he said with no remorse.

It would have to do. Richard knew he would get no better out of Nick. "Why did you take the money? Do I not give you enough? I am twice as generous with you as the others are with their apprentices."

"You make me work for it," Nick mumbled.

Richard finally heard his regret. He was not sorry for what he'd done to William, but he was sorry he got caught. "Just tell me why. You owe me that."

Nick paused but appeared to realize he had no option but to speak. "I have a debt."

"Where?"

"A Pye Corner stew. There was a particular girl. I left London owing them but a little when the plague numbers rose. I didn't know they were usurers as well as bawds."

Being lied to and stolen from was hard enough. Richard was not prepared for this.

"You've been sleeping with whores?"

"She was a clean one," Nick promised. "No risk to you. She wasn't cheap."

Richard had never loved Nick, but they were friends. He hadn't expected it to end this way. Given their introduction, however, he should have known better than to trust Nick. He might like to think he'd rescued the youth from the shadowy world of espionage, but habits picked up in that line of work were hard to break.

"Keep the angel to pay your debts, and here is another for you until you find work," he muttered, handing over some from his own purse. "Now go to my room at the Spurre, take your things, and get as far away from me as you can. I don't want to see you again."

Turning away, he heard Nick drop the coins into his purse and leave. With no argument, Richard knew he would find him waiting at the inn, but the coming protest would be in vain. He had wanted more than Nick could give him for a while, but convenience and money kept them together. For him, at least, there would be other men.

Richard looked across at Geoffrey, who had begun his expletive-filled monologue again, and then at William, who chewed his lower lip as it curved into a wide smile. He appeared to have got over his earlier humiliation extraordinarily quickly.

"Could you not wait until the end of the run?" Geoffrey asked, though he had no reason to support Nick. "We need him for the performance tomorrow, if nothing else, and you won't get the others out of the taverns tonight to sort out a different play."

"He stole from us. You know he can't stay after that."

"I'm not sure that's what is bothering you."

"We are not forgiving him, no matter how convenient it would be. They'd all be dipping their hands in the takings. One of the others can play two parts. Whoever is the least drunk come morning can learn the extra lines."

"I could do it," William said suddenly, his voice high, excited.

Richard was surprised by the interruption as much as the suggestion. "You?"

"Why not? How hard could it be?"

Though Richard was sure William meant no insult, he was not impressed. "You? You're not pretty enough to play a girl."

William was quite breathless now and ignored the slight. "I won't let you say no. I'll jump on the stage tomorrow if I have to. I really want to be an actor. I've been in plenty of plays back home."

"Forgive me, but your village probably doesn't see much quality theater. London tastes are more refined, and you are not acquainted with them. You've only been here one day."

"But I've been watching you for more than a year. Let me show you what I can do. If I'm terrible tomorrow, then I will go home in shame, but if I'm good, you must make me your new apprentice."

He was full of determination. That was something, but Richard's mind came back to his sweet, nervous stammer. Could that be overcome?

There was only one way to find out. "If I think you're going to be terrible tomorrow, I won't let you on the stage. I won't stake my reputation unless I'm sure you can perform, but I will give you a chance to prove yourself. You're coming with me tonight, and we will rehearse and make you ready. Let's see if you're any good."

William grinned, apparently thrilled with the way the afternoon had gone. At least someone was. Richard was a pound poorer and had lost the man who was his lover, apprentice, and friend. With the stress of preparing this stripling for the next performance, he couldn't even muster the strength to pretend to match his pleasure.

He signaled that William should follow him, but Geoffrey said, "Cousin, wait! This may seem fortuitous, but—"

"I am just meeting the terms you gave me." William spoke over him, waving away his interference. "You said I should take any position that becomes available."

"And what position do you think he's going to put you in?"

William flashed him a wicked grin.

Richard felt Geoffrey's words like a knife in his heart. "What I do in the dark never bothered you before."

Geoffrey had the decency to appear guilty. "Your bed doesn't bother me, but he's my family."

"And now my apprentice. I will take care of him."

"That's what worries me."

Richard had half a mind to have William just to spite Geoffrey, but right then it wasn't in him. "Fear not," he said. "I haven't the mood for that sort of mastering."

Nodding his thanks, Geoffrey wiped his brow. His relief disappointed Richard. He had never expected that sort of judgment from his friend.

"Good luck, William," Geoffrey said. "Your future rests on what you accomplish on that stage tomorrow. Don't forget it. I will bring your things to Richard's room later." He left the stage.

Richard and William were alone.

"You will not regret this," the lad promised merrily, his happiness rendering him oblivious to the mood.

"I'd better not. Even if you are wonderful in rehearsal, if I let you onstage and you stammer your way through, you will cost me a lot more than your upkeep."

William smiled slyly. He appeared to be choosing his words carefully as he said, "I'm not nervous, though I may be clumsy my first time. But how can I fail when I'm learning from the best?"

Clumsy? That was an interesting choice. Richard wondered at his provocative tone and his newfound confidence. Was he outside the barn that night, hiding in the shadows? It was best not to ask too early into their partnership.

"Flattery will earn you no more cash from me, but respect will keep you in a job. You may have been watching me for a while, but I've only known you a few hours. We're not friends, you and me, no matter what you might hope. I will be your master."

"An apprentice may like his master even when he is being instructed, if the work is enjoyable," William mused. "And the master ought to like the apprentice. He has to spend much time and effort on him."

"That is a good point. Keep me content. You saw what happened to the last when he didn't."

Dropping his voice, William said, "Teach me well, and I'll keep you more than satisfied. I'm your apprentice, not a whoremaster."

Where does a shy country boy learn to talk like that?

Richard reminded himself that the company's repertoire was full of that sort of language, and let the lad down gently. "Given your earlier blushes, I imagine you know better how to promise than to perform. I will not hold you to your word."

William's happy confidence faded. "I'm not worldly, but I am eager. You may hold me if you wish."

William was tempting. Richard looked into his eyes and saw an intensity that aroused desires he did not wish to satisfy that afternoon. Virgins had their charm, but he'd never truly enjoyed taking one to his bed and didn't prize them the way other men did. That said, the lad's look told him they'd lain together a hundred times already in his dreams. He wasn't as innocent as he first appeared.

"We have a busy afternoon." Richard turned away. "Let me show you our room, and then we will begin rehearsals."

CHAPTER THREE

WILLIAM COULD have danced back to the Spurre. Having spent the first night there, sharing a pallet with Geoffrey's snoring, seventeen-year-old apprentice, he'd begun to wonder if he'd made a mistake coming to town. Now his doubts were gone, and he felt immensely proud that less than a day after his arrival, he had secured a position as Richard's apprentice and made his intentions known to him.

That Richard had not immediately carried him off to his bed seemed only a minor problem. They had only just been properly introduced, and it would be unseemly not to wait until they were better acquainted. At least a few hours ought to pass first. They were about to embark on a love affair, not a quick fumble.

They didn't talk until they stood outside Richard's room.

"If you want to please me, stay here and don't speak," Richard said. He positioned William in the corridor, against the wall, before opening the door.

William watched him.

Richard paused in the doorway, irritation on his face. "I asked you to leave, but I find you here undressed and in my bed. Shall I tell the innkeeper to toss you out naked?"

Nick's voice carried through to the corridor. "You don't want one last fuck? All told, I've had a pound from you today. That's got to buy you something."

"Dress." Richard didn't move.

The conversation paused, Nick scrabbled around for his clothes and his belongings. "Please don't turn me out. I've nowhere to go." He sounded desperate, but William felt no sympathy for him and couldn't wait for him to be gone.

"It's your own fault," Richard muttered.

Nick's voice was close and quiet as he said, "I love you, Richard."

"No, you don't."

"I do. I swear I love you."

"You never lied to me about your feelings before!" Richard barked. "Don't start now."

Nick pushed past him and hurried down the corridor toward the stairs. He was half-dressed, his auburn hair a tousled mess on his head. Despite his desperation, he wasn't crying.

Richard watched him round the corner and then, with an apparent change of heart, called out, "Wait, Nick!" before dashing after him.

William knew he was supposed to wait, but he'd already lost one night to Nick. He wouldn't lose any more. He padded quickly and silently down the corridor and came to a halt at the corner, where he could hear them both clearly on the stairs.

"Take this ring," Richard said in a low voice. "It's not a love token, nor is it to be melted down or sold. I want you to pawn it and bring me the ticket. Slide it under the door if I am not here, but make sure you bring it back to me. Try and buy yourself into a proper trade with the money. Don't go back to peddling secrets or your arse. And get yourself a wife. Men may have money, but we've hearts too. I don't want you leading on a man who is softer-headed than me."

Quickly William returned to his spot by the wall and waited for Richard, who followed a minute later. He looked tired rather than upset, but that was little better.

"Now, we have work to do," Richard said, opening the door again. "We'll get you in costume and make sure your appearance as a woman isn't totally laughable. Then we'll talk through your lines."

"Are you all right?" William asked, following him inside.

"My reputation is about to rest on you and your unknown ability. Forgive me if that gives me unease."

"I'm asking about Nick."

"He was just a distraction. Not worth feeling heartsick over."

Worth sticking your cock in, though.

William was very glad to see the back of Nick.

He glanced around the room. It was a small space compared to his family home, but he thought it generously sized for two occupants, being twice the size of Geoffrey's. Richard obviously expected to make good money now he was back in London. A fireplace stood to the left of the door, a bed to the right, and straight ahead were a table and two stools, arranged next to a large window. On the table stood a pitcher and a bowl, but beyond that, nothing was lying about. William's gaze returned to the bed, where he noted good-quality sheets, though they were rumpled and yellowed with age. He wanted to wrap himself in them and breathe in Richard's musk.

A heavy-looking chest sat in the corner. Richard hefted a golden silk gown from it. The garment must have cost three times what they had made that day. For the first time, William—who had been in countless feast day plays over the years and thought himself well prepared for a life on the stage—was intimidated by the job he so desperately wanted.

"Strip," Richard said. Reminded of the other thing he desperately wanted, William eagerly complied. He didn't allow his disappointment to show when Richard continued, "I'll dress you."

It took a while to get into the costume. The unfamiliar clothes were heavy, and William needed Richard's help. His new master was all business, averting his eyes as William slipped into a smock but helping him with the many undergarments he would have to wear on the stage.

Richard laced the bodice tightly, without compassion, and would not listen to complaints. "Women manage this daily," he said. "You'll live."

Despite longing for it in the past, it felt unnatural to dress as a woman, and William took no pleasure in it until Richard looked him up and down approvingly.

"I take it back. You are quite attractive in costume. You'll be the envy of every Puritan, no matter what they pretend."

William looked down at the dress. The gown hid the hard lines of his body, but his shoulders were no less broad and his large feet peeked out from the bottom of the skirt, which was a touch too short.

"I don't feel girlish."

"You don't look it yet."

Richard rested his arms on William's shoulders and pulled the ribbon from his hair. The dark locks fell free, and Richard tousled them before arranging them about William's face. His fingers lightly brushed William's neck, and William couldn't help but shiver.

Meeting his eye, Richard acknowledged the response to his touch with nothing more than a disapproving look. "Ideally you'd wear a wig, but you won't be playing nobility tomorrow and can make do with your own hair, even if it is a little short."

Next Richard inspected William's face, stroking his fingers across William's smooth cheeks and chin.

William had no hair there yet, which had been a source of displeasure for him in the past, but now he was grateful for it. Richard's fingers were gentle compared to his own rough, work-worn hands, and he fought the urge to lean into the caress. All his attention must be on his performance tomorrow if he wanted to make Richard his permanent lover.

"We will not need to shave you yet, but once we do, you will not have long in skirts."

Richard disappeared back to the trunk and returned with a small box that contained three little pots. He removed two—one rouge, one kohl—and lightly painted William's face before standing back and inspecting his work.

"You could not pass for a real woman. Here." He handed William a mirror. "Your thoughts?"

"I'm not beautiful."

"Most girls aren't, and men struggle even more."

William inspected himself again. He might not have fancied women, but he knew what a handsome one looked like, and it was not him. Nick made a pretty girl; even Francis said so.

"I'm not good enough, am I?" he lamented, handing back the mirror.

Richard looked at him gravely for a moment and then chuckled at his misery. "You'll do for the stage. The crowd will not be so close, and your paint will be thicker. Besides, they like to see you're a man. Everyone knows what they're dealing with then."

Richard wet a rag and roughly scrubbed the rouge from William's cheeks and lips before starting a more delicate cleanse around his eyes. "Keep it on no longer than necessary; it's not good for your skin. White paint is the most expensive, so we only use it for playing royalty, and you will not need it tomorrow. If you're lucky, you may not play girls long enough to wear it. God only knows what I will do with a bearded apprentice, but I suppose there will be servants enough for you to portray."

That was a more comfortable proposition. The only possible advantage to the female roles was the opportunity to be kissed by Richard during the play. "What sort of woman will I be playing tomorrow?" William half expected her to be a nun.

"Minor nobility, unmarried. A country girl."

William vaguely knew the type. He didn't mix with that class, but he'd seen them. She would be a little haughty, despite knowing her place, and she would be playful. As an unwed woman of that breed, he believed she would be as chaste as him. Not that he intended to remain pure much longer. Once the idea was in his mind, he couldn't avoid the question. "Will you kiss me?"

Richard cocked his head, and for a moment, William thought he saw the ghost of a smile. If William had looked away for even a second, he would have missed it and only seen Richard's disapproving glare.

"It is part of the script. You are here to focus, remember, not to beg me for kisses."

"I was asking if it would happen tomorrow, not if you would kiss me now. But thinking about it, we should practice."

"Practice kissing?" Richard snorted. He appeared to be going for derision, but his eyes twinkled merrily. "I should have thought that was natural enough."

"To a man who has been doing it twenty years, I am sure it is. However, as you know, I'm just beginning."

"Have you honestly never even kissed a girl?" Richard asked, incredulous.

"No. Nor a boy neither."

Richard raised an eyebrow but made no comment on that. "Let me show you how your character would like to be kissed tomorrow."

William's stomach fluttered violently. This was the moment he'd waited his whole life for. He puckered his lips slightly, the way he'd seen girls do with their swains, and leaned forward eagerly.

Richard smirked at him and leaned in close.

His lips left the faintest brush on William's cheek, and William wasn't sure they had touched at all. "Is that it?" he asked, pulling himself back upright.

"You didn't like it?"

It would have thrilled William if he didn't know Richard could do better. "That's not how you kissed Nick today," he grumbled.

"That was a different play with different characters. He was my wife. You will play a virtuous country girl who has nothing but her chastity and her dowry. She's not going to give up one without the other."

"I expected more."

"Your problem is that you're a country boy, not a girl." Richard laughed. "Men will always expect more, no matter what their experience. You need to feel your character's desires and put aside your own."

Clearly Richard didn't know a thing about women. "Are you sure she doesn't desire you to kiss her on the mouth? I've stood next to women at your performances who would attest otherwise."

"On this I am firm. A kiss that was any more forceful would not be welcome, even if she finds herself desperately in love with the giver. Think of her like our fair Queen Elizabeth: the only terms she will accept are her own."

William huffed but offered his cheek again. "Go on, so that I may react with more affection."

"No."

"No?"

Richard wore an evil grin now. "You're annoyed. That's good because she will be too. Focus on that and remember the feeling. We're going to try a range of emotions. Ready?"

Unsure what he meant, William nodded anyway.

"Good. Now, give me joy."

Richard looked at him expectantly, but William hadn't a clue what to do. "I don't understand."

"If you want to be an actor, you're going to have to present a range of emotions. Pretend to be joyous."

William remembered the moment he found out he was coming to London. He beamed broadly and bounced on his heels, clapping his hands together.

"That was tolerable, but you need to exaggerate for the crowd. We'll try a few others."

They went through a range of emotions, and William performed as asked.

Richard sat on a stool and reeled them off one after the other, giving him a fair amount of time to think about and try each one. "Anger. Happiness. Misery. Contentment. Aggression. Passion."

William paused longer than usual.

If I show you passion, one of us will not be able to sit down for a week.

Was this a test of his focus? "I can't do it," he muttered, disliking the feeling of being toyed with.

Richard was sympathetic. "Just show me in your face. I will not judge or laugh at you."

"I don't know how."

The sympathetic look was replaced by a frown. "I know you've seen less action than Queen Bess, but you have shown me you understand passion as well as I. How old are you?"

"Twenty."

"Twenty! You look it too."

William didn't know whether that was a compliment, so he made no comment and hoped Richard wouldn't let him go for being too old.

"You're the oldest apprentice in England," Richard continued. "If you're twenty and anything like I was in my youth, then you've known your own hand a thousand times, and probably a lot more. You know passion."

"I don't know what it looks like. I'm not thinking about my face."

"What are you thinking about? Wait—don't answer. You're blushing, and that's not what we want."

A knock at the door interrupted them. "Come in!" Richard called.

Geoffrey opened the door sheepishly. He dipped his head in greeting to William, not blinking at the sight of him in female garb.

"What is it?" Richard asked impatiently.

"Here are the lines and my cousin's few things." Geoffrey set his load down on the table and stood awkwardly beside it.

"Thank you. I'll see you tomorrow." Richard refused to look at him.

"Please, Richard, don't be like this. Can I speak to you? Alone?"

Richard shook his head but then relented. "Stay here," he said to William. "Don't even think about stepping out of the room in that

dress unless you want to earn a coin from one of the other tenants."
He left for Geoffrey's room next door.

William hurried to the wall and pressed his ear against it. He could hear nothing. It didn't matter. He had a fair idea what was being said and would wager his cousin was playing the dog in the manger, warning Richard off again. He would die a virgin if Geoffrey had his way, and right then, when he was so close, William could think of nothing worse than that.

It was harder than he imagined, being near enough to touch Richard but not being able to. Geoffrey was only making it harder. It seemed impossible to focus on a job he would like when there was a man he would love, and William's thoughts were consumed by Richard alone. Reminding himself that only hours had passed since they'd become properly acquainted and he might have to wait days, or even weeks, until Richard gave in, William knew he should give up teasing himself with playful banter. More direct action was required, and if that didn't work, he would just have to wait.

For a moment, he felt peace, knowing he had something of a plan in place. Then he dashed over to the window to see if he could hear better from there.

CHAPTER FOUR

"I've NOT touched him, if that's what you're worried about," Richard muttered as he stepped into Geoffrey's room. "You don't have to worry about me turning him into a sodomite. He's halfway there of his own accord."

Geoffrey winced. "I know what he is, all right. He made no secret that he was coming here for your bed, and I brought him regardless. In all honesty, I don't care what he does, and if he likes the company of men, then let him have it. Even better, let him have it here in London, where word won't get back to his mother. But you and I have known each other for fifteen years, and you have called almost as many men lover. I can think of only one you truly cared for at that."

"What exactly is your point?"

"I don't want him heartsick over you in six months' time when you have moved on to a new man, or worse, back to an old one, and left him regretting he ever fell into your arms. He won't take a pallet next to the bed while you have a stranger in his place. When you and he are finished, he will be gone. This is his one chance to be a success. I don't want him to squander it."

Richard did not like the way Geoffrey painted his character. He'd lain with many men, but he didn't just toss them aside when they were done. His lovers were his friends; they regarded each other as convenient bodies, and emotions weren't often involved. He never understood why woman-lovers felt at least one person in the bed should have a tender heart, especially when society did not often expect it to be those men.

That was not to say Richard hadn't been in love. He'd loved long and deeply in his time and had even been as amorous a youth as William. Yes, he knew love, but many years had passed since he'd felt that way about a new man, and with the fresh disappointment of Nick in mind, he was not disposed to fall in love again now.

"Our relationship will be that of a master and apprentice," he snapped, "and any man I have known in the past is nothing to do with that."

"You were master to Nick for a few days too before he got into your bed."

"That was not a love affair. It was an opportunity for him to increase his allowance and an arrangement for me to enjoy myself occasionally without having to go looking. There were no feelings involved. You know Nick is incapable of loving men."

Geoffrey took a seat at his table and huffed. "We are not talking about Nick. William has his head and heart filled up with thoughts of you, and he will make it easy for you if are feeling lonely one night. I'm just asking you to bear in mind how simple it will be to let go of him afterward. If it will cost you nothing to end it, then it might be best not to start, for his sake."

As aggrieved as Richard felt, he knew there was truth in that. If William believed he was in love, then better for Richard to maintain his distance. He didn't play with men's emotions, and he didn't appreciate when others did. "I won't break his heart," he promised.

"Thank you. He's young. I'm sure his ardor will diminish, and you can do what you like with him then with my blessing. Just promise me you'll wait. The only other person I know who needs an apprentice is Will Shakespeare, and he's randier than you are."

Richard left feeling a little better about his friend's interference. He returned to his room and found William slumped on the bed, still wearing the gown.

"Get me out of this," William grunted. "I leaned out the window, and a wag offered me a penny for a suck."

Richard laughed and hauled him up to unlace the back of his bodice. "A whole penny? You must look expensive in this dress. What did you say to him?"

"I was too stunned to speak. I just shut the window."

"Next time tell him it's a groat to see your ankle, and he couldn't afford the rest. What were you doing leaning out the window anyway?"

"Nothing."

William replied far too fast for that to be true. Richard guessed he'd been trying to listen to the conversation in Geoffrey's room, and let it go.

William was quickly naked—and now there was no shirt to cover his modesty.

Richard made a point of not looking, but he was aware of creamy skin and something darker hidden among a bush of black hair. Strangely it was more exciting that he couldn't stare. While William had been enticing before, having sworn off him made him temptation itself.

"Rare organization!" Richard said, turning away from the sight and snatching up the script from the table. "You're in luck getting your lines a day early. You can read?"

"I've had schooling." William didn't appear to be in any hurry to dress.

"You've not seen the handwriting yet. It's just your lines. We'll do a read-through tomorrow at the theater, and I will rehearse with you this evening. Learn it well, I'll test you in an hour." He thrust the paper into William's hand and then hurried to the door.

"Where are you going?" the lad asked, seeming slighted. "I thought we had work to do."

"For this part, you will work far better without my distraction."

Richard left the room and let out a sigh of relief before heading down to the bar for a drink. He needed it, but he was mindful that he ought not to have too many. Even with the day he'd suffered, knowing a willing youth was in his bedroom would be too much of an invitation to mischief.

The tavern was as crowded as ever. The Spurre had long been one of the most popular in town, doing double duty as an alehouse and a brothel. Women plied their trade openly, leaning against the wall, tits already out, waiting for a buyer, but you had to ask at the bar if you wanted a man's attention. It was rough, but Richard had called it home more than once in London, and he liked it.

As he walked through the throng, he caught snippets of gossip. Lord Strange was dead, a victim of the Catholics' fondness for him, if the tavern talk was anything to go by, though many a man had died of a stomach malady without being poisoned. Richard had met him numerous times and admired the man for his lack of political ambition. Strange was a lover of the arts above all else.

The notion of a plot intrigued Richard, but he let it go. Not even the death of an acquaintance could compel him to dwell on the machinations of the day. A nice, quiet life, that was all he wanted these days.

Of more concern was what it meant to the other playing companies. There was no Lord Strange's Men without the earl as patron. Will Shakespeare would be looking for more than an apprentice.

Richard spied a table in the corner with a single stool and sat, then called over the serving girl to fetch him something to eat and drink. He'd been expecting to feast tonight, but as Nick had cleaned him out, it would be simpler fare. After ordering a mug of ale, cheese, fruit, and some bread and butter, he sent the same up to the room. It should guarantee William was clothed when he returned.

What a pity William was Geoffrey's cousin. If he'd been just another admirer who'd taken a fancy, Richard would have obliged him with a turn in his bed. Even if Nick hadn't betrayed him, he could have fitted William in. It would be nice to lie down with someone more interested in his body than his purse.

Thankfully he was back in London now, which meant plenty more opportunities for a fuck if he wanted it. The men of the provinces were far more cautious than those in the city. Here bedfellows were easy to come by, especially south of the river. Vice was a given in Southwark.

His food soon arrived and he tucked in. As he was finishing up, a familiar figure entered the bar, and Richard reflected that he should have taken his chances with William in his room.

Bennett Goldfox ordered a cup of French wine and approached with a smug expression. He was nearly fifty now but still handsome. His clothes, cut to the latest fashion and trimmed with green velvet, were expensively tailored and a perfect fit to his hard, tight body. He fenced, which kept him in excellent shape. Bennett could hold his own with men twenty years younger. Nevertheless, his hair and beard had taken on a fetching silver tone, and he had lines around his eyes and across his forehead. Despite Richard being thirty-four years old, looking at Bennett made him feel like a boy.

There were no greetings or pleasantries, although more than a year had passed since they last met, and that had not been a fond farewell. Bennett simply took an empty stool from the nearest table, sat next to Richard, and said, "I heard about young Nick."

Probably from the lad himself.

Richard wondered if Bennett came to commiserate or crow. "It's all right," he replied nonchalantly. "I've already moved in his replacement."

"That's unlike you."

"Someone has to play his part tomorrow, and this one is a keen apprentice."

"You know that's not what I meant."

Richard knew, all right, but he hadn't wasted any love on Nick. The betrayal made no difference to his need for a new apprentice.

"I took him on as a favor to Geoffrey. He's his cousin."

"Oh."

At once Bennett wrote William off, and his dismissive tone annoyed Richard. Despite his better judgment, he found himself boasting. "He doesn't look like Geoffrey. He's incredibly handsome."

"That's not unlike you at all, then, apart from the timing. You normally let the sheets cool first."

"I'm not heartbroken, if that's what you're thinking. A little disappointed, but I was under no illusions about Nick. You must have known he wasn't interested in any more than the money when you introduced us."

Bennett gave a small nod, the slightest acknowledgment of the truth. "You were together so long I assumed tender feelings must have grown between you."

Only friendship, and Nick had spat on that when he stole and he lied. The bawds didn't help. Richard didn't fancy a dose of the pox and rarely stooped to the stews himself. He'd expected the same of Nick.

"You know two years is not long for an apprenticeship, and Nick would have had another three if he'd respected me enough to be honest with me. I'm sure this new one will last longer than that."

Bennett sipped his drink, and Richard ignored him as best he could. He didn't want to be openly rude, but Bennett must know he was not welcome. Richard had spent his plague-enforced exile trying to forget him, but here he was, acting as if they'd never been apart. It annoyed Richard, and he ignored the tiny corner of his heart that was pleased to have been sought out. After so long apart, Bennett should have forgotten him. It would have made things much simpler.

"So what is he like?" Bennett asked.

Richard had already admitted William was attractive and was now regretting it. "He's fresh out of the country," he said casually. "Looks, manners, charm…. It won't last long in London."

"Not living here," Bennett commented, then took a sip of his wine, trying to hide his amusement with the cup. When he put it down, he asked, "Can I meet him?"

Richard busied himself with the last of his food. "There's no point," he said, cutting into a stewed apple. "I might be kicking him out tomorrow if he performs terribly."

"On the stage or between the sheets?"

"I'm not getting involved with another apprentice. Not after the mess Nick left us in. You know what that's like."

Bennett nodded again, and Richard could not meet his eyes.

"You didn't have to release him," Bennett said gently, as if he spoke to a child. "And it's not too late to take him back. He knows he did wrong, and I doubt he will frequent the brothels again. I suspect he will even be a little more affectionate, if that is what you need. I could arrange it and pay his keep."

All Richard needed from Bennett was to be left alone, and that comment confirmed it. "I did not release him for sleeping with whores. I let him go for stealing from the company. He had to leave, and the other sharers won't want him back, no matter what incentives you provide. Now, I've got to go test the new lad on his lines."

Richard left the table without a good-bye and returned to his room with his heart pounding. They had met more than fifteen years ago, but Bennett still possessed the power to shatter his confidence.

Upstairs he found William seated at the table by the window, eating and drinking while he pored over the script in the fading light. He'd donned his stockings and breeches, no doubt because one servant had seen him naked and he didn't want to risk another, but he had left his shirt off. The air was cool and he looked cold, but Richard wouldn't make him cover up. The sight of his chest was just the right amount of flesh. Richard could endure and enjoy the view without desiring any more from the young man.

William gave him an inviting smile. He nodded to indicate a second stool, which he'd placed next to himself.

Richard moved it to the other side of the table before he sat. "Do you know your lines yet? I'm about to build the fire if you need more light."

"I think I've got it, though you might need to confirm a few words for me, and I'll need my cues," William replied as he scanned the page again.

William's speed was impressive, but Richard didn't show it. Some days his new apprentice would need to learn his lines even faster, and with ten different plays being staged over the next two weeks, he would have to get used to the pace.

Indicating the modest platter, Richard asked, "Do you need more food and drink? Country appetites seem to be so much larger than here in London, and a yeoman's son must eat well there."

"I am satisfied. The only thing I miss is our family honey."

"We all long for something sweet occasionally."

A knock at the door interrupted them. Assuming it was Geoffrey again, Richard rose and went to the fireplace. "Come in!" he shouted as he threw some wood onto the cold hearth. "I was just about to ask you for a spill."

The door opened, and Bennett chuckled. "Richard, we have known each other a long time. When have you ever known me to carry a flame?"

The words bruised, but Bennett's appearance at his door was much worse. Richard should have known better than to think Bennett would respect his wishes and leave him be. Downstairs he had been polite, the public setting holding his tongue, but this was an insult, and he would respond to it. "What are you doing here?"

Bennett looked upon William with obvious appreciation. "I've come to greet your new apprentice. He's comely, just as you promised."

Richard glanced at William, who'd stood to greet their guest. William smiled at Richard rather than Bennett, blushing at the compliment, although it hadn't come from Richard's lips.

"I told you not to come up here," Richard snapped, turning his attention back to Bennett.

"Yes, but I thought you might want my help. You have often needed it in the past. Besides, I'm sure there are a few things I can teach him."

Jealousy joined anger in Richard's breast. "He is learning lines. There's no need for any assistance from you."

"And what does he have to say on the matter?" Bennett gestured to William, who stood silently.

Richard was grateful William knew better than to speak before he was asked, even if he was the one being discussed. "Answer him, lad, but talk little, as we've work to do."

William hesitated only a moment, and then, lowering his eyes, he said, "I thank you for your interest, sir, but my master's teaching is adequate."

It wasn't the most glowing review Richard had ever received, but *adequate* would do. "There you have it. Now you may leave."

Bennett remained unfazed. He always put on a good show, even when he was under the deadliest of threats, and this would be a mere trifle to him. "I will go, but not until I am sure your apprentice speaks for himself rather than his master." He stepped toward William and looked over his body admiringly.

William kept his eyes turned to the floor, and Richard could tell the gesture was born from unease as much as deference now.

Bennett treated William like an animal he intended to bid for at auction—circling him, checking him from all angles, and nodding approval when he saw something he liked. "Does he even know what he is turning down? Can he tell where my interest lies? Has he considered how I would have him lay?"

William looked up, alarmed, and Richard stepped between the two of them, putting his hand on his dagger.

"You cannot buy this one."

It was no threat at all. "Why not?" Bennett sounded genuinely confused. "You don't want him. You said so yourself but a minute ago before you left me downstairs. And where will he sleep if not in your bed? If you're going to be as generous with him as you were with Nick, then he ought to work for it."

"I asked you to leave," Richard said firmly, hand still on the dagger.

"As you wish, but first let me share the reason for my visit."

Bennett took his purse from his belt and removed Richard's ring from inside, proffering it to Richard. "Nick sold me this. I thought you might like it back."

"Keep it."

Bennett slipped the ring onto his finger and admired it as if he might keep it after all. When he removed it, he held it out to Richard again. "I always did like this ring, but I gave it to you in good faith once before, and I do so again now."

Richard couldn't remember Bennett ever being good or faithful the last time he received it. "I care not for that trinket. I wouldn't have given it to Nick if I did."

"You told him to pawn it. Are you honestly suggesting you had no intention of buying it back?"

"None. I intended to send the ticket to you in case you wished to reclaim it."

Bennett's ever-present smile faded, and Richard knew he'd hit his target. There was no glory in the victory. Despite himself, he wanted the ring, and it had cost him dearly to part with it.

"You're angry at me now, but I know it meant something to you once," Bennett said quietly, putting it down on the table.

"That was a long time ago."

"Maybe your new apprentice would like it instead."

William found his voice before Richard could speak. "Thank you, sir, but I will accept tokens from no man but my master. My loyalty is to him alone."

His defiance matched Richard's, and Richard turned around in surprise to look at him. William was breathing heavily, eyes blazing with anger. The stupid boy would get himself in trouble if he kept it up.

Bennett wasn't used to hearing that tone from anyone but Richard, and his face betrayed his bemusement. "Perhaps I was wrong," he murmured, reappraising William. "You might have your money's worth yet."

He left them alone.

When he was gone, Richard could not stop himself from taking the ring and slipping it onto his finger. "Go get a spill from Geoffrey so we can light the fire. And put your shirt on."

William didn't move. "Who was that?" he demanded.

"An old friend."

"You weren't very friendly."

Richard looked down at his ring. "That's because I was trying to protect you."

"From what? Does he think I'm a whore?"

"Not exactly. You weren't offering, but he wanted to buy you."

"Pig," William muttered. Richard found himself chuckling bitterly, but the lad still frowned. "How do you even know a man like that?"

"There was a time when I called him master."

"He's an actor?"

"A goldsmith."

A dimple of confusion appeared on William's brow. "You were training as a goldsmith, and now you're an actor? That's a bit of a step down, isn't it?"

Richard had fallen further than that. "Don't we have work to do?" he asked irritably. "I told you to fetch a spill."

"But—"

"I'm your master, William, not your friend, and you're certainly not my confidant. Get the fire lit."

William snatched up his shirt and hurried out the door without a word.

Richard felt a sliver of guilt and tried to let it go. He'd spent much of the afternoon pretending to be in a better mood than he felt, and he was tired. William should get used to that. But Richard remembered the man he was at twenty, and determined to do better by William than Bennett had done with him.

Richard was a performer, quite used to feigning happiness when he felt misery. He wouldn't let his apprentice find him so tense when he returned.

CHAPTER FIVE

GEOFFREY WELCOMED William in and offered a spill immediately, but William didn't have the will to light it. Instead, he warmed himself by Geoffrey's fire, in no hurry to return to Richard's room. Geoffrey sat on a stool next to him, reading a chapbook in the firelight. When he reached the end of a page and William remained, he observed, "You're in no hurry to return to your master. Are you no longer enamored of him?"

William didn't answer, posing a question of his own instead. "What sort of man is Richard?"

"It's a bit late to be inquiring now."

"I know, but I need you to tell me honestly what you think of him."

Geoffrey fidgeted in his seat and did not offer an answer straightaway. William was expecting the worst until Geoffrey confessed, "He has his share of faults, as all men do, but he has been a good friend to me, and he's a real talent on the stage. You wouldn't find a better man to instruct you, save myself, of course."

"But what sort of man is he?"

"Not a bad one. I've known him fifteen years, and I've been in business with him for almost as long. He's loyal and brave, and many times I have been proud to call him friend."

"Hmm."

Geoffrey heaved himself up from his stool. He put a strong hand on William's shoulder in support. "Has he rejected you?" he asked gently.

"He has neither sworn off me nor made love to me, but I've more than that to mind."

"Remember, William, he's just a man. On the stage, he may have seemed a god, but here, in the least reputable inn in Southwark, you may see his lowliness."

William did not care about that. The company his master kept concerned him, but his ill temper had really stung. Hearing that Richard didn't want him hurt most of all.

Thanking his cousin, William lit the spill and left. In the hallway, he wondered if he should have mentioned the visitor, but he didn't know the man's name.

Silently he entered Richard's room and lit the fire. They both stood near the fireplace as they waited for it to take, and for a few minutes, neither said a word.

Eventually, his tone conciliatory, Richard said, "We should rehearse your lines now."

So William buried his feelings and got on with it. Richard made only a few suggestions, and they ran through their scenes three times. He seemed pleased when they were done, all tension apparently forgotten, but William was unable to share his pleasure.

When Richard went downstairs to fetch them some ale, William took the opportunity to learn a little more about his new master. He went first to the large trunk and dragged out the paints and costumes before he found a packet of papers underneath. He riffled through them hurriedly but found only plays and receipts. Quickly he replaced everything, glad the trunk wasn't neatly kept, and then looked around for Richard's personal effects, which he could not see. He was looking under the bed when Richard returned with the drink.

"What are you doing?" Richard asked as he entered the room. He looked confused rather than suspicious.

"Looking for a comb."

"Under the bed?"

"Mine has broken teeth. I was looking for yours."

Richard handed him the tyg of ale and pulled back the chest to reveal his bag stuffed behind it. "Here," he said, tossing the bag over.

William rummaged inside. He could feel a leather wallet among the assortment of things, but he already knew he wouldn't go back to it. If Richard trusted him enough to show him his hiding place, he must have little to hide, and nothing William felt in there was worth the risk of being caught. He took the comb and went to sit by the fire, where he ran it through his hair.

Richard took a seat next to him, leaning back against the edge of the table. They both watched the flames.

"You're doing quite well, lad," Richard offered. William assumed that to be high praise. "Do exactly as you did tonight at the performance tomorrow, and you will be fine. Are you nervous? It's difficult speaking in front of a crowd."

William had been acting in plays since he was a small child and had never been nervous in his life until he was confronted with Richard. Even that passed when William set his mind to having him. Now he felt overwhelmed for the first time. He had believed he could do anything to get Richard's heart, but after the evening's events, he wasn't so sure.

"I'll be fine," he replied numbly. Out of the corner of his eye, he saw Richard turn to look at him.

"What's wrong?"

"Nothing."

Richard snorted. "Terrible acting. You will have to do better."

"Nothing is wrong."

"Any more of that and I'll release you too," Richard continued playfully, but his voice wavered a little, and William could tell he was still on edge.

"Nothing. Is. Wrong."

"That was the worst yet."

"Then release me," William shot back, the words out of his mouth before he could stop them.

Richard took the comb from his hand. "All right. Geoffrey won't like it, but if you leave now, then that's not my fault. You are free to go. Thank you for wasting my time when I could have been training someone who does want this job."

William wanted to act and to live in London and to be with Richard. He just didn't want any more of the treatment he'd received that evening. "I do want to be your apprentice," he mumbled.

"And yet you are so quick to quarrel with me," Richard snapped, but he caught himself and suppressed his temper. He took a deep breath through his nose and let it out again slowly. "I'm sorry I was short with you before. It was not aimed at you. Bennett frustrates me."

So that's the bastard's name.

"Why?"

"He wanted to turn you into his whore. I didn't like the way he spoke about you."

William hadn't liked it either, although at first he'd enjoyed hearing he was comely. No one had ever told him that before, but he couldn't admit that to Richard.

"What do you care?" he muttered. "I have all but offered you a tumble, and you're not interested. Should I have no man at all?"

It was not a question William intended to have answered, but Richard replied, "There are men enough in this world that you do not need Bennett. I would like you to find someone as young and disposed to love as you are. Enjoy your youth. Don't throw it away loving an old man like him, or me, for that matter."

They watched the fire again in silence. The room was dark but for the orange glow of the flames, and William was glad of it. He found himself embarrassed by Richard's words and was grateful the dark hid his red cheeks. That Richard considered him little more than a child wasn't a surprise, but he'd hoped that wouldn't matter. Nick was twenty years old too, and Richard had taken him to bed every night.

No, it couldn't have been his age, rather his lack of experience. "I've made a fool of myself," he murmured.

Richard looked across at him again, and even in the shadows, William could see he was surprised.

"You have enticed me no end, and I never met a fool who did that. You're young, not stupid. Nevertheless, do not take my words as inducement to continue. I would break your heart if you let me."

A chance of a broken heart would be a fine thing. William had been in Richard's employ for several hours now, and already he was growing frustrated with the slow progress of their relationship. His head knew it would take time, but his cock, which was a willful beast now it finally had its chance, had its own ideas.

"I thought there were a few times you were encouraging me," William said, trying to make it sound more a statement of fact than an accusation.

"I was, but that means nothing. I like playful talk. It passes the time."

So Richard was a tease. It was no more than William deserved. He had been leading on girls for years. "I was sure you fancied me, and because of that, I've let my prick lead me around. My vanity is the only problem here."

"You do not seem vain. And you are pleasing to my eye."
More teasing.

"You were the one who said I wasn't pretty enough."

Richard hummed as if he were considering his previous words, before offering, "You're pretty enough for the stage in that dress, but prettiness has never attracted me. Right now you're handsome. That's more where my interest lies."

William felt a stirring in his loins. Despite the disappointments, despite the distrust, his body still longed for Richard, and this last confession made him forget all else. "So you do like me?" he asked hopefully.

"I don't dislike you." Richard sounded less sure of his words this time. "I want you to be confident, that's all. If circumstances were different, I would have bundled you into my bed hours ago. But I am your master, and you saw how it turned out with the last apprentice I danced in the sheets with."

William had no designs to visit bawds or steal. Richard's body was the only thing he desired. With his cock aching, he knew only one way of getting what he wanted that night, and he grabbed for it.

"I should go back to Oxford." The words tumbled from his lips before he had time to think of the consequences.

Richard let out a growl of exasperation. "Perhaps you should if you are going to change your mind every few minutes. You're lucky Geoffrey is your cousin, because I would throw you out right now if he weren't. Now, do you want to act or not?"

That wasn't the response William hoped for, but he persevered regardless. "I'd love to act if I am able, but I'm not here to be an actor. I came to London to get close to you."

"And here you are, in my room, living as my apprentice. It's the closest I will let you get. Don't throw away your chance in life because you want a grope with me."

Of course he was right, and even William's heart agreed that in the long run it would be better to stay and wait Richard out. He wanted a love affair, but his prick wouldn't be ignored any longer. They were both willing, both able, and the way William saw it, only Geoffrey's interference kept them apart. He would get Richard into bed even if it ruined him.

"That's not why I came to London. There's no point staying if I can't have you. I'd rather have one good night and leave tomorrow than spend a lifetime waiting for it."

He expected another argument, but Richard appeared to have had enough and accepted immediately.

"As you wish. You may go free tomorrow after the performance. You've done this work, so you might as well get your payment."

William was free again, which was a frightening thought, but he would worry about getting his apprenticeship back in the morning. Now they were no longer master and apprentice—they were just two men whom circumstances had brought together.

He took up the tyg and downed his share of the ale. Handing the cup to Richard, he feigned a yawn. "I want to lie down. I'm ready for bed now."

Richard continued to stare at the fire and said nothing. He had more resolve than William allowed for, but that didn't mean he wouldn't give in when William was lying naked next to him.

All William needed to do now was find an excuse to be in the bed. He looked first for the pallet before he realized Richard didn't have one. "There's only one bed."

There was a long pause before Richard said, "We will have to share."

William felt his cock twitch. This was it.

Richard stood and followed him to the bed. William stripped off quickly while he watched him in silence. Richard didn't look away this time and stared straight at William's prick as it jutted out from his body, long and thick and full. Richard looked hungry for it, and in that moment, William was ridiculously proud of his manhood.

Richard made no move to touch him. William reached out and took his hand, but Richard pulled it back.

"I should not be doing this," Richard said, voice hushed. "I gave Geoffrey my word that I would not touch you until I was sure."

"Sure of what?"

Richard didn't reply.

"Please," William said, stepping closer to him. He rested his hand on Richard's chest and then ran it down between his legs. He felt his stiffness even beneath the padded fabric of his trunk hose.

Richard closed his eyes. "The serpent in the Garden did not offer so much temptation," he muttered as he picked William up and tossed him down onto the bed before climbing on with him, still fully clothed.

William reached for Richard's doublet and began to unfasten it—no easy task as his hands trembled quite violently now it was finally happening. He was a mixture of nerves and excitement, and he couldn't stop himself shaking.

His lover gentled him, taking one hand in his own and reaching out to feel his shoulder with the other. "Are you cold?" Richard asked, concerned.

For Richard to think of his comfort at a time like this had to be a good sign. "Not a bit," William promised. "I'm feverish right now, and you must be hot too. We should get you out of these clothes."

Richard's brow furrowed, and he pulled away slightly. "You're trembling. Are you afraid?"

"I love you," William whispered, "and I'm in your bed. I've nothing to fear."

With that confession, Richard let go of him abruptly. "I'm cold. I think I'll go and sit by the fire some more." His voice carried a forced gentility, but William could hear the tension in it.

"Did I do something wrong?" He grabbed hold of Richard so he could not leave. "Show me what to do."

Softly, Richard pushed him away. "It is your youth, that's all. You've done nothing to be ashamed of."

"I'm untouched. Any mistake I made can be put right if you teach me. You see how I need your mastery?"

Looking down at William's cock, which remained stubbornly hard, Richard said, "I see it, all right, but I've let myself toy with you enough. You played your part perfectly, and soon, when you've done with wanting me, you will be making men unbelievably happy. Only a fool would refuse you."

Richard left the room in a hurry, leaving William alone in the bed.

That was it, his one chance, and he had ruined it. Tomorrow afternoon he would have no position, no lover, and he would have to walk back to Oxford, work the farm, and, when the time came, find a wife. It was over.

William curled into a ball. He didn't cry—he liked to think he was tougher than that—but he did feel very sorry for himself.

CHAPTER SIX

DOWNSTAIRS AMONG the crowd of drinkers in the inn, Richard found himself looking around for Bennett. A mixture of anger at his old master and a need to find a bed for the night drove him.

He knew how it would go. Bennett would accept his complaints, maybe apologize if his mood was right, and then welcome him into his arms. Richard wouldn't need to work for it, pay for it, or feel guilty about it afterward. Yes, Bennett would be most welcome, for once.

But he wasn't there, so Richard sat in the corner and drank himself into oblivion.

When he awoke the next morning, he found he was in his bed. William slept next to him, still naked beneath the sheets. A quick check confirmed he was still clothed, although his doublet and shoes had been removed.

Richard dragged himself from the bed, went to the privy and then the bar, and returned with a jug of watery ale and some breakfast. There was a thin smear of honey on William's bread, and Richard eyed it queasily, having the stomach for naught but dry toast and the weak drink. He set it out on the table and waited for William to wake before eating.

When the lad roused, he looked surprised to see Richard there with the spread.

"I didn't think you'd be up before noon," William muttered, rubbing his eyes.

If only they had that luxury. "We'll need to be at the theater long before then for rehearsals."

William left the bed and dressed silently. He wasn't concerned about hiding his body, but there was no seduction in his nudity either. He approached the table and sat in front of Richard without comment.

Richard asked the question he had been dreading. "What happened last night?"

Glaring down at the food, unable to even look at him, William replied, "You came to the room swine-drunk, were sick out the window—

which you left open, by the way—and then climbed into bed. You were asleep moments later."

"I'm sorry," Richard said, and he meant it. He could have handled the whole evening a lot better.

"What have you got to be sorry about? It's your bed."

"I should have controlled myself. It's not a comfortable night next to a drunk. I won't let it happen again."

"It doesn't matter if it does. I won't be here tonight."

Richard had accepted William's talk of leaving the previous evening because he hadn't honestly believed William would go. He was good at spotting a play, and he was sure the lad was making one. It suited them both to pretend William was leaving, and even when they were on the bed, Richard never intended for him to quit.

"You don't have to go," he offered. "We can put last night behind us."

"There's no reason for me to stay." William picked up his bread and took a bite. He jolted as he tasted the dab of honey and inspected it closely before taking another mouthful. "Thank you for breakfast," he said quietly.

Richard only managed a few morsels before he passed his toasted bread over to William. Watching him eat, he thought upon the things he could do to win the young man's good favor again. He must find a way to make William stay. If he didn't, Geoffrey would be angry, Bennett smug, and worst of all, he would feel guilty that William had thrown away such a valuable opportunity over him.

But William wasn't comfortable making conversation or even looking him in the eye right then. Richard let him think. He might feel different when it came time to go.

They walked to the theater with Geoffrey and his apprentice, Thomas. Their partnership was based purely on business, but they seemed to like each other well enough. Thomas was rarely around when they weren't performing or rehearsing, kept to his curfew most nights, and caused no trouble for his master. It was the perfect working relationship. Richard couldn't help feeling slightly envious of them.

In spite of that, when he compared the two apprentices, he knew whose company he would prefer. William might be hard work, but

Richard was finding him increasingly irresistible. Beyond his looks and his country manner, he was a reminder of Richard's youth. That was undeniably attractive.

Backstage at the theater, they changed into their costumes, and Richard painted William's face. He was delicate with the makeup again, mindful of its value. He just softened the edges as he'd done the day before and let William's long hair hang about his face.

All the while, William remained quiet, eyes down, speaking only when he had to. Richard began to worry as the time approached, but when they stepped out onto the stage, William was confident, and he acted his part well. That he was playing an angry, rejected lover might have helped.

Their two characters moved swiftly to a happy ending. Through the course of two hours, among the other twists and turns of the plot, they came to a position where they might be alone together. That was when Richard was supposed to steal his kiss and win back the fair lady's heart.

In rehearsal he had been chaste, but that would not do now. William needed a reason to stay, and as Richard looked across the stage at him, he realized what it was. He approached swiftly, snatched William into his arms, and kissed him full on the mouth.

William's whole body stiffened in surprise, but then he relaxed and took the kiss willingly, opening his lips to let Richard delicately explore with his tongue. He tasted of the sweet honey and ale he'd breakfasted on, but his faint moan of pleasure made him truly delicious.

Richard kissed him deeply but not passionately, mindful it was his first time and they were on stage in front of a crowd. It could not last forever. Releasing William, Richard stepped back and looked at him, waiting for his line.

William didn't speak. Instead, he licked his lower lip and then, narrowing his eyes, slapped Richard hard.

The blow was bad enough for being unexpected, but the force behind it was astonishing. Richard stumbled backward, clutching his hand to his face.

William grabbed hold of him and kissed him again, more forcefully than the last time. Now William was in control, and Richard could do nothing but accept the intensity of it. He felt himself stirring. If the lad had done that last night, Richard wouldn't have left him alone.

The crowd was cheering and laughing when William finally let go of him. The actors took their bows and walked off the stage.

"I need to teach you how we do that without actually making contact," Richard said, rubbing his cheek as they stepped out of view and into the back of the theater. "That's more like it, though. You gave me passion, all right."

"That's just what I was thinking," William said, his eyes alert, cheer in his voice for the first time that day.

Whether it was the thrill of performing or the kiss didn't matter. He looked happy. Richard would have to be careful now.

"I'm pleased you let your character respond, but did mine honestly deserve the slap?" he asked, thinking that after that kiss, he probably did.

William grinned at him. "You should have kissed me like that last night instead of saving it for the stage."

"I could have done, but then you would have expected more, and your character wouldn't have been so surprised. I wanted *her* to bite, and she did not disappoint."

"You want bite?" William asked and turned to shove him. Richard stumbled back into Geoffrey, who was walking behind.

Richard didn't ask what that was for. That time, he was certain he deserved it.

"That is for assuming you can play with me now," William growled as he walked away.

Geoffrey propped Richard upright, chuckling at them. "You were brilliant, William," he said. "Did you put on a lot of plays while I was gone?"

William ignored the question and snatched up a jug. He wet a rag to remove the paint from his face.

"William?" Geoffrey asked again. He looked concerned.

Richard would have some explaining to do. "Let me speak to him."

"I'll not have everyone know our business," William muttered. "We'll talk in your room before I leave for home."

"All right." Richard relented. He spent the rest of their time at the theater trying to avoid Geoffrey's scowl.

BACK IN their room at the inn, Richard sat on the bed and patted the space next to him, but William hung by the door, not tempted by the position. Perhaps he was serious about leaving, after all.

"I don't expect you to go," Richard said simply. "You have talent. You could make a good job of this if you stay. I must confess also that I enjoyed being on stage with you this afternoon."

That was as much as he could safely say without lying to William or leading him on.

William bit his lip, but he didn't move even a step. "Will I remain your apprentice?"

"Yes, for a few years. When that is done, if you have the means, you can buy a share in the company, and you might become a moneyed man. It would be unfair not to remind you this is your best hope to make something of yourself. You're too old to apprentice elsewhere, and no one else will take you for free."

William stared at the floor and appeared to consider Richard's words. Then he approached slowly and sat next to him on the bed. "You're right; staying is the sensible thing to do, but my heart has no sense at all, and I must think of that too. The kiss on the stage… it was nothing like I was expecting. For a moment, I thought that…. You have to tell me, will there ever be night work?"

Richard couldn't help himself, and he chuckled. "I'll not pay you any more than I paid Nick, if that's what you're asking."

William remained deadly serious. "Do not mock me. I need to know if there will ever be more between us, even if it's just kisses."

There might be more, one day, if William's heart cooled or Richard's grew warmer, but how could Richard explain that to him? Better to keep William's expectations low and avoid disappointment. "There will be plenty of kisses every day on the stage for the next few months, if you want them."

"Want them? Have I not risked enough to show you? I have been in love with you for more than a year. I'd wait all season for you to arrive, and every time I saw you, I loved you a little more. I'll stay for the kisses, but I want to rehearse them in your bed."

William's words were heartfelt, that was obvious enough, but Richard didn't want to believe he truly meant it. The passions of youth were the strongest, but they were also the most fleeting, and built upon the weakest foundations. William wasn't the only one with a heart to break.

"You are as sweet-savored as you are sweet-faced, and you know I am tempted. More than tempted, even—I could not lie to you about that. I will admit I enjoyed kissing you, and you felt my desire for you last night, but you barely know me, and I know you not at all. You would not love me if you understood my character. I am only decent enough not to promise you a love affair that might not last."

William stood and looked down at him, putting himself in the position of power. He wasn't listening; Richard had seen the change in him when he admitted again that William tempted him. Beyond that, William appeared to hear nothing.

"I know all I need. My body aches for you to touch me. Isn't that love?"

Richard laughed again, though it was gentle, not mocking. "It is not. That is lust, and it is a far more unruly emotion." He couldn't help himself as he continued, "Nevertheless, it's often where love starts."

"You lust after me, don't you?" William asked, lips curling into a smug grin. He was playful again now he believed he might get somewhere.

Richard looked him up and down slowly, too weak to pretend he didn't want the lad. "I'm not blind. I've been lusting after you from the moment I saw you, and that is no exaggeration."

"So you may fall in love with me soon enough if you give in to your craving for my body?"

"And you may find that when you've satisfied your desire for me, you feel nothing."

"It would be foolish not to find out," William whispered as he climbed onto Richard's lap and kissed him.

The trembling was gone. After the kisses on the stage, William was as confident as any of Richard's other lovers.

Richard fell back onto the bed, pulling William down with him. He knew he should stop this, but he couldn't. All he could do was hope Geoffrey wouldn't find out.

The bed creaked beneath them as Richard rolled over and on top of William. Pulling away from the lad's lips, he placed kisses on his jaw, then his neck.

"Lower," William moaned, pressing upon Richard's shoulders, trying to force him down his body. "Or give me your hand at least. I'm going to burst."

It *was* the lad's first time. Richard shoved his hand down into William's hose. There he found his prick hot and hard, the skin velvety smooth, the tip wet. He gripped it and gave him a tug, which elicited another cry of pleasure from William. After only a few more pulls, he stopped, knowing William would come off if he did not. Instead, he pushed down farther, running his fingers lightly over William's tight balls and toward the crack of his arse.

He would not enter William, not his first time and not with a dry finger, but he wanted to touch him there and had thought about it a great deal the previous night when he was filling his cup downstairs in the bar. It was a promise to both of them of what was to come, but right then, William didn't seem interested in it. That was all right. Richard liked to give and take, and if William wanted to give, he would happily take it all night.

"My cock," William begged. "Touch my cock again. I haven't come off in a week."

Before Richard could move his hand, a loud thump on the door interrupted them.

William froze in his arms. "Who's that?" he whispered, alarmed.

"I'm busy!" Richard shouted at the door.

There was another loud thump and then another, and another.

"I said go away!"

The banging stopped.

"They're gone." Richard went straight back to his work, finding William's cock and giving him a strong stroke to bring him back into the moment.

William gripped Richard's shoulders tighter, gasping for breath. "Do that again," he pleaded.

It would be over in seconds if he did. Richard hesitated, and William thrust into his hand, groaning. The lad was so close. If Richard wanted more, he would have to pull his hand out now, but he couldn't do it. He looked at William, finding his cheeks flushed, face showing the deep concentration he needed to hold his seed back. When their eyes met, William smiled. He was comely before, but now Richard thought he was one of the loveliest men who ever graced his bed. Passion suited him.

"What are you doing?" Geoffrey barked as he shut the door behind him.

"Cousin!" William gasped, all excitement gone. He pulled away from Richard and scrabbled backward along the bed, yanking up his hose as he moved.

"William!" Geoffrey exclaimed, even more surprised. "They told me Richard had a whore in here."

William was too embarrassed to be insulted.

Richard moved in front of him, protecting him from Geoffrey's disapproving glare. "I was just persuading William to stay," he muttered.

"Of course you were."

"What are you doing walking into my room anyway?"

"There's a man in the hallway demanding to see you."

"So? Send him away."

"I'll send him in," Geoffrey huffed. "William, with me. Now."

William, still embarrassed, didn't argue. He went to the door silently with his head down, but he looked back at Richard and winked when Geoffrey wasn't looking.

Geoffrey opened the door, and before they could leave, a tall, fair-haired, thickly muscled man pushed past them without a glance and entered the room. Richard didn't know his face, but he could tell from his manner that he was trouble.

"He's all yours," Geoffrey grunted as they left.

He may only have been an actor these days, but Richard could fight like a soldier with sword and dagger. His fists, however, were another matter, not gentlemanly enough to have bothered learning. He didn't fancy his chances in a brawl.

His weapons lay across the room, and he couldn't get to them without raising suspicion, not that he even wanted them. Richard had enough blood on his hands.

There was a time when he wouldn't have hesitated, when the dagger was never out of arm's reach, but he was not that man now, and he hadn't been for a long time. He'd only had to fight for his life once to understand that it was no way to live.

No, he was not a spy, not anymore, and he wouldn't behave as such in front of this man, whoever he was. Too many years had passed for him to believe this visit had anything to do with that despicable part of his life, even with all the little jobs he'd somehow ended up taking on in exchange for a bit of warmth from Bennett.

Besides, his cheek was painful enough after the slap from William, and he didn't fancy finding out what the man might do to him if he provoked an attack. He didn't imagine it would be as pleasurable as what had followed with the lad.

"Good day," he said, as if such an interruption were nothing. "How can I help?"

"Are you Richard Brasyer?"

Richard's heart sank even further. He'd found himself in far worse situations, but his adversaries didn't normally know his name.

"'Tis I."

"I'm here to collect a debt."

Richard sighed, a mixture of relief and resignation. "It wouldn't happen to be owed by a man calling himself Nick Smythson?"

"I don't know his full name, but Whoreson would be more appropriate than that. All I know is he's a talkative fellow who likes to gamble, and he claims he's connected to someone that can pay."

"How much does he owe you?"

"Fifteen pounds."

Richard was anticipating a sum in shillings and wondering how he might pay that. Fifteen pounds was beyond anything he could have imagined. "How much?" he asked, shocked.

"Sixteen pounds."

"I thought you said fifteen!"

"It's twenty now."

"What's going on?" Richard demanded.

"Thirty pounds. Any more questions, and it will get higher."

Richard shut his mouth. He had plenty of questions, but nothing to pay for them with. As he couldn't afford thirty pounds, what did it matter if it ended up at a thousand? But he knew where he could get the money and pay it back on good terms.

"I can get you thirty pounds tonight," he promised. "I will meet you in your place of business—wherever that may be—in three hours, and we can swap, the money for Nick."

"Your young swain is long gone. That's why we're after you for the money. I will collect before your show tomorrow, at the door, one minute before you are due on stage."

Richard opened his mouth to protest, but the man continued, "It would be expensive to try and negotiate, and even more expensive to attempt to follow me. Now, I'm going to have a drink in the bar. I expect to see you leaving shortly."

Silently Richard nodded and watched him go.

"Oh, Nick," he murmured as he sunk down on the bed, "what have you done?"

This was bad for him, but it might be much worse for Nick, even if Richard could pay.

William entered moments later and hurried to embrace him. Richard stood quickly, thinking it better they stayed off the bed. He could not afford to give the lad ideas right now.

"I watched for him through the keyhole in Geoffrey's room," William said, squeezing him tightly. "Who was that man?"

"I'm not sure, but he claims Nick owes him, or whoever he's working for, a lot of money."

"How much?"

"More than I have."

William stepped back and looked at him, straightening his back and shoulders and raising his chin. "I'll protect you," he said gallantly. "He's big, but I've got three brothers. I've been fighting for years, and I'm pretty good with my knuckles."

Richard knew the truth of that. His cheek still smarted. "There will be no violence. I can get the money. I need to see Bennett."

"The whoreson who wanted to buy me?"

"That's the one. He will lend me the money. I guarantee it." An open purse had always been one of the few things about Bennett that Richard could count on.

"Is there no one else? Perhaps Geoffrey could give it to you."

Remembering the furious look on Geoffrey's face a few minutes earlier, Richard didn't expect Geoffrey would give him a friendly word, let alone thirty pounds.

"We've been out of London two years, eking a living from the peasants in the provinces. Even if all the sharers banded together, we could not afford this debt. Besides, they wouldn't pay for Nick's folly, and I wouldn't ask them to."

"So you must grovel at that bastard's feet?"

"He won't make me beg." Richard took up his bag from behind the chest again, ignoring William's grumbles about Bennett's character. "Stay here for an hour. That scoundrel is drinking in the bar downstairs, and if he sees you, he might think you'll make a good hostage. Let him finish, then go get yourself a good dinner." He found his purse and took out a penny. "Here. You may spend it all. Bennett will feed me."

William looked down at the coin in Richard's hand. "You're very sure of all the things Bennett will do," he murmured.

"I was younger than you when I met him. He is incapable of surprising me."

William pocketed the money and then stepped closer so he could kiss his cheek softly. It brought a fresh sting to the slap, but Richard didn't mind.

"Don't be long," William whispered. "I'll be waiting for you."

There was so much promise—too much—and Richard had already gone too far. He kissed William's lips, because he could not stop himself, but the sensible part of him hoped William would be asleep when he returned.

CHAPTER SEVEN

WILLIAM STOOD at the window and watched Richard walk up the road. As soon as he rounded the corner, William went to work, flinging open the lid of the box and rummaging through the costumes for a suitable disguise.

Having no idea where he was going, he dressed in a clean, but rather plain, brown doublet with white hose, and found a hat large enough to hide his long hair underneath. He hoped he wouldn't appear suspicious in the smarter parts of town or look like an easy target downstairs in the bar. Looking down at his outfit, he guessed he got it right and prayed the brute, whoever he was, hadn't noticed his face.

When William stepped into the bar, he was pleased to find the bastard still there, sitting comfortably at a table finishing his drink. William left the inn and walked out into the busy street to wait for him to leave.

Immediately he recognized his mistake. In the Spurre, he could have sat and waited with a drink, but loitering outside could draw the wrong sort of attention. Looking around for a reason to remain, he saw the man who'd shouted up to him at the window the day before. He would fill a few minutes.

It was easier to think of him as a would-be suitor than a potential customer, and although the man would be neither, William approached him as such. They were of an age and fairly matched in both height and build. The man was a costermonger, used to humping his basket of seasonal vegetables around the streets, which built his muscle the way farm work had done for William. This must be his usual patch.

The seller's skin was tan despite the time of year, and he had a smattering of freckles across his face. His black hair was cut short, with small wisps curling tightly against his head. William was most struck by his full lips, which curved into an unselfconscious smile as he approached. William wondered why someone so handsome needed to pay for a man's attention when he could probably get it for free if he looked in the right places.

"Hoy! I remember you!" William called, crossing the street to greet him. His tone was playful and friendly, knowing what the seller believed him to be.

His suitor grinned at him. "I've not forgotten you either, even if you are more politely attired today."

William glanced over his shoulder at the tavern door and positioned himself where he could get the best view. "I thought you were going to come knock for me."

"You looked like you'd have knocked me out if I did."

"I was scandalized," William teased. "A penny for a suck? That's not how you talk to a lady."

The young man laughed. "You're new around here, aren't you?"

William silently chastised himself for not bothering to hide his country accent, but it was too late now. "New to London, but not to my job," he bluffed. "Where I come from, you wouldn't say that to even the lowliest woman in the street, let alone a man. If you saw something you liked, then you ought to have come up."

"How would I find you? You're not the only pretty boy in a pretty dress in that fine establishment. You should have given me your name. What shall I call you?"

William was beginning to regret the encounter altogether now, having no desire to tell the costermonger his name. The youth was attractive and would have caught William's eye in Oxford, but he wasn't Richard. "Let's talk plainly," he said as he sidestepped the question. "I don't care what you're called, and you don't care what I'm called."

"I might care," the seller replied, and William could tell he was wounded by the refusal. "My name's Sam, if you're interested."

William wasn't. "You offered me a penny. My name's much more expensive than that, but I'll wear any name you like for no extra charge."

"Just make sure you wear the dress too," Sam replied with a wink.

At that moment, William's target walked out of the tavern. Resisting the urge to show his relief, he promised, "One day. I'll lean out the window when I'm ready. Right now I've errands to run."

He gave Sam his friendliest smile and turned to go, but Sam caught his arm and pulled him back.

"Hold on. When can I come see you? Are you busy tonight?"

Shrugging him off, William replied, "Not tonight, but soon, I promise. Now I really do have to go."

The sinking feeling in his stomach told William that was the second mistake he'd made that evening. He would have to get Richard to warn Sam off—gently, because he seemed nice, and the attention was flattering. William wasn't yet sure how he could explain to Richard what he'd been doing trying to convince a handsome stranger he was a bawd, but he would, no doubt, think of something.

William had to hurry down the road, as the man he followed was moving at speed. The road had no twists and turns, and the scoundrel didn't look back to see if he was being pursued. Clearly he was confident his work was done.

At least one of them was. William didn't know London at all. He could find his way to the theater and back, having walked it a few times now, but he had no idea where he was headed currently. After he crossed the bridge, he took note of landmarks—an interesting shop sign, stocks, a tavern—hoping vainly he would be able to see them in the dark on his way back.

To his surprise, he eventually found himself in a more respectable area than he'd imagined the brute would lead him to—a long, wide street, lined with printers and binders. The shops were closing up, but William could see a bookshop on the corner was still open. He judged from the direction they were taking that this was their final destination, but something didn't seem right. What would a man like that be doing there?

William had to take a chance. His gut told him that was the place, and he hurried around his target and rushed into the shop.

"Can I help you, good man?" the elderly shopkeeper asked. He looked decidedly unthreatening.

"I'm looking for chapbooks," William mumbled, unsure of himself, not for the first time. At least if he was mistaken, he would come to no harm.

The bookseller pointed to a pile of pamphlets on a table and watched him browse. Then the door opened, and in stepped the scoundrel.

It took all of William's effort to remain as casual as possible. He looked up briefly, as anyone might, then turned his face back down to the chapbooks and listened to the conversation.

"That was quick," the bookseller said. "I thought I might be here long into the night waiting for you."

"He made it easy. Didn't push the price of the book up too much; didn't follow anything up."

"You're sure?"

"Someone kept an eye on him for me."

"So we can close the deal tomorrow?"

"I believe so, but plans may change. More support might be required."

"Go out the back, and we will discuss that."

Obviously they were talking about Richard, but William wasn't entirely sure of the details. Had he not known the man's former whereabouts, he would have assumed they discussed an expensive book and thought no more of it.

"Excuse me, young man," the bookseller addressed him, "I'm about to close. Do you want to buy something?"

William put down the chapbook he was holding and shook his head. "I need a better look. Are you open tomorrow?"

"Noon until sundown."

"Then I'll be back tomorrow afternoon."

He left the shop, heart pounding with excitement or relief, he could not tell which, and began his journey back to the inn. The light was failing, and he hurried, knowing he might lose more than his way if he didn't get back soon.

All the while, his mind turned over the information he had gained. This was something more than mere extortion, he was sure of it, but what, he could not say. Perhaps Richard would have a better idea.

Night had long since fallen when he reached the Spurre, but he had kept to the main streets and made it back safely.

Sam was gone, replaced by drunken brawlers who spilled out from the inn. William pushed his way inside and to the bar, where he ordered a jug of ale, a bowl of mutton stew, and a generous portion of bread to have in his room. He was so relieved to be back, he at first didn't notice Geoffrey sat watching him.

His cousin approached as he carried his food through the crowd. William groaned, thinking about the lecture he was about to receive. Geoffrey had been completely silent earlier when William waited in his room, which was the best indicator that he was very angry indeed. Now he looked ready to unleash it.

Geoffrey stepped ahead and held the door for him to pass into the back rooms. "Where have you been?" he growled.

"I went for a walk," William replied casually, grateful Geoffrey hadn't immediately launched into a speech in the middle of the bar about the virtues of chastity.

"You went for a walk at night?"

"The sun was shining when I left. Richard has gone out, so I decided I'd make the most of my free time and explore my surroundings."

"In one of the company's costumes?"

William was all innocence. "Is that not allowed? I won't do it again."

Geoffrey rolled his eyes. "Come on, up to the room. You need to get that doublet off before you spill stew on it."

Geoffrey navigated as they walked upstairs in the dark. The main corridor was faintly lit by small pools of orange firelight that peeked through the cracks in the doors. They soon entered Richard's room, and William sat at the table to eat his dinner while Geoffrey built up the fire.

"You should go back to Oxford," Geoffrey muttered as he worked, not bothering to look at William. "Have your night with Richard, make the most of it, and then go home."

William had been expecting Geoffrey would try to send him back, and he was ready to argue. "Why leave?" he asked, as if he'd done nothing wrong. "I love it here."

"Your prick loves it here."

"My prick, heart, and head are all in agreement."

"For now, but can't you see the danger he's put you in by sending you out spying?"

"What do you mean spying?"

Geoffrey looked over his shoulder at him. His face was in shadow, but William could hear his confusion as he said, "You know, going out looking for information."

"Richard gave me a penny for a good dinner and told me to wait in the room for an hour before I could get it. He didn't send me anywhere."

"So why have you been out in disguise?"

"Because I wanted to know what's going on. I hoped I would discover something useful that could help Richard."

"And did you?"

"I'm not sure. I didn't find what I expected."

Taking a seat on a stool at the table, Geoffrey silently watched him eat. Eventually he said, "Don't put yourself in danger again. Not for Richard."

William hadn't considered the danger. He thought only of his burning curiosity and the delight he would see on Richard's face when he returned with information.

Moreover, he had no reason not to believe Richard deserved his trust. Well, no reason except the reputation of actors in general, Geoffrey's initial warning, the behavior of his former apprentice, the even worse behavior of his former master, and then the criminal who'd interrupted them that afternoon....

Perhaps he had been a little foolish.

But he was glad he'd done it. Richard's resolve not to have his body might be crumbling, but more would be required to win his heart, and that was William's next target. Besides, it was fun, thrilling even. He liked playing a spy.

"You told me yesterday he was a good man," William reminded him, clinging to the one thing Richard had to recommend him.

Geoffrey huffed, unable to deny that. "He is a good man, one of the best, even, and I would trust him with your life. But I wouldn't trust his associates. His past is a little more colorful than yours or mine, and apparently it has caught up with him again."

"This isn't about his past. That man was here to collect Nick's gambling debt."

"Did you confirm that on your travels?"

William did not want to admit he had not, and so said nothing at all.

With a heavy sigh, Geoffrey said, "I know you think you love him, but if he cares about you at all, he'll make you go home. He won't want you to get hurt."

Geoffrey was right, but even if Richard ordered him out of his life, William couldn't go back to the village. If he returned now, he might be comfortable until his father died. After that he would find himself eking a living off a small plot of land, ending up married to some woman he hadn't the stomach to lie with, and wishing he was in Richard's bedroom, truly living.

He wasn't going to be frightened, not when everything was going his way. Better dead in London than waiting to die in Oxford.

"There's nothing for me there, and you know it. Here I have a trade, a lover, and the potential to improve myself immeasurably."

"And the potential to get yourself killed if you go sneaking around at night. Even Richard would tell you that. Where is he, anyway?"

Good question. How long did it take to collect thirty pounds and eat a bit of supper? Surely he would be in a hurry to get home after their earlier interruption.

"He's gone to get the money Nick owes from some man called Bennett."

Geoffrey dropped his head and rubbed his eyes. "Bennett Goldfox," he muttered. "This gets better."

"You know him? Richard said he was apprenticed to him as a goldsmith."

"That's right, he was."

"So how did he end up an actor?"

"That's none of your business, and if Richard won't tell you, I certainly won't," Geoffrey snapped.

"Can you tell me about Bennett at least? He came here yesterday, and I didn't like him."

"Maybe you're a better judge of character than I thought," Geoffrey replied wryly. "It sounds like you know all you need to about him. Suffice to say that you'd like him even less if I wasted my breath on him."

William had a lot more questions but knew he wasn't about to get any answers from Geoffrey. Not sober, anyway. "This is so miserable. We're cousins—we shouldn't be fighting like this. Go get yourself a jug of ale and keep me company tonight. I might make mischief otherwise."

Geoffrey raised a disapproving eyebrow but then appeared to relent. "Save your mischief for when Richard gets home. I'll treat you to something special, and then it will be time for those London tales you wanted to hear back home. You're a man now. I suppose I should be grateful for that."

William watched him leave and then went back to his stew. He wasn't quite a man yet, but Richard would be back later, and they would finish the job. All round, it was going to be a good night.

Geoffrey returned a few minutes later carrying papers and a candle, but no jug. "Your lines," he said, placing them on the table. "Here's your first tale of London. You work your arse off, and you don't get to relax until you're done. We've a performance tomorrow, remember."

William pulled the script toward him and squinted at it in the firelight. He grudgingly admitted he deserved this, and he knew he would be thanking Geoffrey in the morning.

CHAPTER EIGHT

BENNETT'S HOME was impressive even at night. Richard arrived just after darkness fell, to find the expensive redbrick house looked no different from when he last left it more than two years ago. The building was a miniature palace; not to say it was small, only that the carved cornerstones and the large windows were grand beyond its scale. It featured all the latest architectural fashions, boasting three expansive curved gables and intricate strapwork weaving across the walls. Richard had been little more than a boy when it was being built and was dazzled by it before he ever knew the owner.

Somehow it suited Bennett to call such a place home. He could be ostentatious within his circle, but he was wary of attracting too much attention from outside quarters. Wealthier than many of the gentry, Bennett could afford a much larger house if he chose to ascend to their ranks, but the relative modesty of an eight-bedroom property, even one so lavishly turned out, granted him something much better—a place in the hierarchy he wished to maintain. Not too low, not too high. To Bennett, wealth and power were measured by more than the number of acres a man boasted or his status at court.

A servant immediately let Richard in as if he were expected. He had lived in this home on two separate occasions, and he assumed Bennett still made it clear to his employees that, should Richard call, he could come and go as he pleased.

He waited in the library, which was brightly lit with beeswax candles and a roaring fire—as was every public room in the house. Bennett probably still had a chandler on staff. Either that or he was singlehandedly keeping one very lucky shopkeeper in business.

Richard sat in a chair at the table and waited. He resisted the urge to look through the piles of papers, knowing nothing of any interest would be left out, and instead studied a map of the Virginia coast spread across it.

The door opened and Bennett entered, casually dressed in tight canions, obscenely short trunk hose, and an unlaced shirt. Richard was struck again by how well his former master had aged. In his midthirties, Bennett had been handsome, and the almost sixteen years they'd known each other had only improved him.

Though Bennett's appearance was relaxed, as if Richard had interrupted him with a lover, he spoke seriously. Closing the double doors behind him, he said, "If you have come to chastise me again, then I assure you I feel extremely guilty. I should not have spoken to your apprentice the way I did, and I ought to have respected your wishes. I'm sorry."

The apology made things easier. It would have been that much harder for Richard to swallow his pride without it. "Thank you, but that is not the reason I'm here."

Bennett seemed surprised and approached now with ill-concealed interest. "It is too much to hope that you call for the pleasure of my company," he said, half a smile already on his lips.

"I do not."

"And I know it's not about that blush on your cheek. I watched the performance today. Your new apprentice has talent and a strong right arm. It looks like that hurt."

Richard touched his face and found lingering warmth from the slap. Although it continued to ache, he didn't think it marked him. "I've had worse," he replied, with more indifference than he actually felt.

"I remember."

Taking a seat on the opposite side of the table, Bennett asked, "What brings you home to me?"

Richard paused, watching Bennett's expectant face. The pleasure Bennett took from this was obvious, but his expression wasn't mocking or smug. For once he looked genuinely pleased to be in Richard's presence. His smile began to fade, however, as Richard remained silent.

"Speak, please," Bennett murmured. "I would hear what has brought you to my home."

"I need your help."

Bennett was visibly relieved. "Whatever you need is yours. What is it?"

"Money."

"That's easily done. How much do you need?"

"Thirty pounds."

Bennett didn't even blink. "You always were expensive." He chuckled.

Richard had taken more than that from Bennett over the years but never in one go. "Blame Nick," he said wearily. "The brothel wasn't his only debt."

"Who would have extended him such credit?"

"The scum who arrived to collect said it was gambling debts, but I don't believe him."

"What do you think it is?"

This was a moment he had been dreading, more so even than when he'd had to admit he needed help. Dropping his voice, he said, "I think he has been talking a little too loudly about your association."

"I see."

Bennett didn't look as alarmed as Richard expected. Given that Nick had visited him the previous day, he might already know about that. Richard didn't press him for information. He didn't want to know what had happened to his former apprentice. He couldn't imagine it was good.

"It may have been a small debt originally, but the man who came to collect quoted fifteen pounds and doubled it before we finished talking. They know he is connected to serious wealth."

"Or they merely believe it. Did you investigate?"

"No, I came straight here."

Bennett seemed surprised. "Were you frightened of him?"

"No. Why follow him now when I can do it after the drop tomorrow? He'll be much less wary of me when he's got your gold and thinks the job is over."

Richard hadn't quite worked out the details of how he would track the man and appear on the stage at the same time, but he would think of something. He hoped Bennett would arrange to have the man followed so he could wash his hands of the whole thing, but Bennett did not offer, and Richard was too proud to ask for that sort of help. Money was tough enough; he didn't want to appear to condone espionage on top of it.

Bennett stood and indicated he should rise too. "Come to my bedchamber, and you shall have all the money you need."

It had gone this way before, and Richard wasn't surprised now. It would have been much worse if he had to work the debt off any other way. He could admit to himself, if to no one else, that this would be immensely pleasurable.

"Am I to start paying it off now?" he asked as they began the short walk to the bedroom.

Bennett glanced at him. His eyes twinkled with delight, and it was obvious he was amused by the suggestion. "You know I keep money in a chest in my room. I'm not taking you up to my bed. If that's how you intend to repay me, then I'll have you be my master-mistress from now till kingdom come."

Thirty pounds bought a lot of fucks. Bennett was right; that would have been too easy.

"I don't want to owe you for long," Richard mumbled. "I might be able to make enough this season to pay you back, if I write a lot of plays."

They entered the bedroom, and Bennett said, "I'm sure there's other work. If Nick has been talking, then we need to discover what is known. My privacy may be at stake."

That was exactly what Richard was afraid he would say. "I can't," he replied, knowing he might find there was no other way.

"Because you'd rather lie in my bed?"

"I'd rather not be here at all."

"I understand," Bennett said, but Richard could see that had stung. "Take this as a gift. You needn't do intelligence work, and I won't expect you to lie down with me. I'll take no pleasure from your body if you take none from mine."

Intelligence work. That must be for Richard's benefit. Bennett had never before had a problem talking about spying.

"I will willingly pay my debt with my arse, my purse, or a combination of the two. Nothing else."

"Then that will have to suffice. There's probably little to learn, anyway. What do you think he's said about me?"

"I've no idea. Hopefully nothing more than that he has a rich lover who will pay up. But you should have one of your men look into it."

"Why? You don't seem to think it's important, and I've always trusted your instincts before."

Was Richard supposed to feel guilty for refusing to investigate? He'd done what he had to—gone to Bennett with the information when he could have protected Nick and simply asked for the money. He didn't have to be the one to go looking. "I told you because I don't want anything to happen to you," he snapped. "So make sure you look into it."

Bennett chewed his lip, and Richard could see his former master was trying to stifle the smile that followed that admission. "You're sure he was talking about me?"

"Who else does he know with thirty pounds lying around?"

"You were doing quite well before you left London," Bennett reminded him with a shrug.

"Not that well."

"Why don't we ask Nick?" The bedroom door was still open. Bennett shouted, "Send up the new boy!" before closing it.

"He's here?" Richard hadn't expected to see Nick again, and to be confronted by him now unsettled him.

"Working in the kitchen. He came to sell me the ring yesterday, and I couldn't let him go into the unknown. He has served me well over the last two years, and I know he was your friend."

There was only one way Nick could have been serving Bennett.

"You had him spy on me?" Richard asked with distaste.

"He didn't have to spy. Nick was as close to you as any man could be. He sent occasional coded letters that he dictated to your unsuspecting cast and then returned to me via my network. I still have the one written by your hand. He told me only the contents of your purse and the state of your health."

There was a knock on the door, and it opened a crack. Nick peered through. He looked guilty.

"I told you to leave London," Richard growled, trying to maintain calm. It was difficult because he was so angry with the lad.

Nick entered, head down, and shut the door behind him. "You told me to get as far away as I could," he mumbled.

"And you could only manage two miles?"

"I have no one else."

"If you treat everyone as badly as you have me, then I'm not surprised."

Bennett ignored Richard and asked gently, "Nick, do you have any gambling debts?"

"No."

"Does anyone know of your former relationship with Richard?"

"The whole of London knows I was his apprentice, and they all say I've been in his bed, though they've no proof. That's all."

"And your dealings with me?"

"I've never mentioned your name. I swear it on my life."

"Good. You may go."

Nick left, looking relieved. He didn't look back.

"It seems you were the target, after all," Bennett said, turning back to Richard. "Nick claims he has told no one, and I believe him. My men would have told me if there were pernicious rumors about us."

It didn't seem possible. "I've nothing to give them. Nick had a pound off me yesterday, and that was all the money I was sitting on. If we were anywhere but London, I couldn't have given him that."

After a moment's thought, Bennett said, "You've money in the costumes. Perhaps only a few of the better gowns would cover it."

"I won't raid the company to pay a stupid boy's debt."

"You won't have to. I told you, I will pay."

Bennett pressed a panel on the wall, and it came loose. Inside was a hollow space with a small chest and what appeared to be a dozen empty purses next to it. He didn't remove the box, simply opened it and began to fill one of the bags. Looking at its contents, Richard guessed the chest was probably too heavy to move.

This wasn't the only hidden chest in the house, but it was one he knew well, and that was probably why Bennett had led him to it. Looking around the room, Richard noted nothing else had changed since he was last there two years before.

"Here." Bennett handed him the purse and then turned back to lock the chest and replace the panel. "Thirty pounds. And five extra for you."

Richard needed the money but knew he couldn't accept it. "Thirty is already a lifetime's earnings for many men. I can't take more from you."

"The rest is a gift. I'll not see you go cold or hungry."

Richard weighed the purse in his hand. "I'm not that poor," he murmured, but his small savings were gone, and it would take time to build them back up, especially with a second apprentice he'd promised to pay twice the going rate. That was what Nick got, and William ought to have the same. William was offering the same terms, after all.

"The money will ensure you remain so," Bennett said gently.

"I can't take it. Let me have my pride."

He handed back the purse, but Bennett immediately returned it.

"You will not meet a single man in the street who wouldn't snatch that out of my hand. Take it. Pride is for the wealthy and the stupid. You are neither of those things."

Richard tied the purse to his belt and didn't argue. "Thank you."

They stared at each other. This was the moment Richard had been anticipating and dreading the most.

During their time apart, he had imagined being in Bennett's bedchamber on many occasions. He had long ago resolved not to return, but each time, a better reason than the last brought him back. Now their business was concluded, all he had to do was thank Bennett and leave. He could not.

"I see you're wearing my ring," Bennett said, breaking the silence.

Richard looked down at it. "I didn't know what else to do with it." When he looked back up, he noticed Bennett rubbing the space on his finger where it had once lived. "I should go. Thank you for your help."

"Wait," Bennett said, although Richard hadn't moved. "Let me hold you again, just once more. It has been such a long time I have forgotten what it's like."

An embrace wasn't unfair, not after Bennett had been so generous. Richard stepped into the warmth of his arms, knowing not to trust him but letting himself enjoy the moment.

"I've missed you," Bennett confessed, voice hushed, as though he was ashamed of the idea.

"It has been too long. It's good to see you again," Richard replied, letting the words he ought to hold in slip away from him. He didn't like Bennett, but he'd missed him terribly.

Bennett held him a little tighter. "You don't have to say it just because I gave you the money."

"I'm not. Your kindness this evening to both me and Nick has earned you the truth. I missed you too."

Bennett chuckled, his hard body moving enticingly against Richard's. "That was worth every penny."

Richard pulled away. He should have known better than to speak freely in front of Bennett. He did know better, but being the idiot he was, he had done it anyway. "I didn't say it for the money," he growled.

Bennett caught his hand and held it. "I'm sorry. I didn't mean to suggest I could buy the sentiment. Not from you. I bought your honesty."

"As you said, I can't afford pride now," Richard muttered, snatching his hand back.

"Then have mine. I am proud of what you have become."

That was untrue. "Good night," Richard said, moving toward the door.

Bennett let him go, seating himself on the bed. As Richard opened the door, Bennett asked, "May I kiss you good-bye?"

"No."

"I understand," Bennett said, a touch of disappointment in his voice. "Good night."

In the hallway, Richard shut the door and leaned back against it. He should be happy. Perhaps he would have been if Bennett hadn't crassly suggested he could buy his affection, but the chuckle mocked him, and the idea that his emotion was based on a bag of coins cheapened him. Given their history, he could not stand to hear it.

Bennett should have just asked for a fuck as payment. He'd never scrupled about buying it before—not that he'd ever directly done so from Richard. Bennett could have his arse for a farthing if he wanted it, and only then if he insisted on paying. He always took care of it.

Bennett had been Richard's first, and in fifteen years, none had bettered him. That was half the reason Richard returned to him time and again. The rest was because he loved Bennett almost as much as he hated him.

And that was the reason he couldn't move now, the reason he was leaning against the bedroom door instead of hurrying away and congratulating himself on a purse of coins obtained at the expense of Bennett's pride. He must have been wounded by Richard's refusal to kiss him.

Good.

But all Richard could think of was the happiness on Bennett's face at finding him in the library, the softness in his voice when he'd admitted to missing him, and the gentleness of his arms clasped around his body.

Perhaps this time….

No, that was Richard's heart talking, and his head knew he'd heard it all before. Richard would not trust him again. He'd revealed his weakness to Bennett the day they met, and it had been used against him too often when Bennett had needed his help. As Richard matured, Bennett worked harder to obtain his good favor, but he'd managed it each time.

Not now.

Richard told himself that, even as he felt his resolve crumbling. He had three choices. One, he could return to William and swear off him for good. That wasn't going to happen. Two, he could return to William, give up his arse to the lad, and rut all night. That shouldn't be allowed to happen, not if he ever wanted Geoffrey to speak to him again. Three, he could stay with Bennett.

When he'd walked away from William the previous night, he had wished for Bennett to distract him from his lust for the lad. Now he was there, outside Bennett's bedroom. Surely that was a sign?

He turned around and opened the door.

Bennett still sat on the bed, head in his hands. "What is it?" he asked wearily before he looked up. Their eyes met, and Bennett's expression turned to delight. "Richard? I thought you'd gone."

Richard hurried to the bed and pulled him up into his arms. He kissed Bennett fiercely and felt Bennett's upper body relax against his chest while farther down his cock stiffened.

"Have me, please," Richard begged through the kisses. "It has been so long since I let a man take me, and that is all I want right now."

Bennett seemed surprised. "You never let Nick?" He pulled his lips away from Richard's and searched his face. He obviously assumed Richard was lying, but right then Richard didn't care.

"With him, it was all hands and mouths, and the occasional fuck when I fancied his arse. I used him sparingly. Now please, enough talk. I need you inside me."

They kissed again. Bennett swiftly unfastened Richard's doublet and pushed it from his shoulders. It hit the floor a moment later, quickly followed by the rest of their clothes.

Richard shoved his lover onto the bed and climbed on top of him. "Where's the oil?" he growled.

Bennett grinned at him. "Where do you think?"

Richard remembered. He reached under the bed, feeling around for it. His fingers brushed the soft carpet, then stroked over a pair of silk slippers and a smoothly varnished box until finally he found a small bottle, which he brought up onto the bed. Pressing it into Bennett's hands, he whispered, "Don't tease me or make me wait. I've had enough of that these past few days, and I just want to come off."

Bennett kissed him before pushing him down onto his stomach and pulling his arse up into the air. Bennett's tongue, warm and wet, slid across his hole. He gasped at the sensation, clawing at the sheets beneath him before he snatched up a pillow and clung to it. There was one more lick, then another, and another. Soon the tongue was joined by well-oiled fingers, and Richard could take no more.

"Please," he begged. "Your prick—I must have it."

Bennett chuckled again, but Richard took no offense.

"Hurry," Richard urged. "Two years' wait is long enough."

"Roll over," Bennett said.

Richard turned onto his back.

Bennett looked down at him, cock hard and leaking with desire. "You will have it," he promised, "but I will not be able to hold back long when I'm inside you."

Bennett's sculpted chest rose and fell fast now, and Richard let his eyes linger on it. The hard muscles were still dusted with dark hairs, long after his head had succumbed to silver. He had the body of a man in his prime.

"How often I have dreamed of you like this," Bennett said, gaze traveling over Richard's body. "Now you are here, I can't make it last."

He snatched up the oil and drizzled it over his cock. After that, everything was a blur as Bennett fell upon him, forcing a kiss onto his lips. Richard felt his lover's prick rubbing against his own, and then it was gone again and Bennett was pushing back Richard's legs and pressing inside.

There was an intense burn, just for a moment, as his body stretched to accommodate Bennett's impressive cock. Then it touched him in a place he had no name for, a place that felt like the very center of his being. He closed his eyes and moaned at the joy of it, the spark of pleasure igniting his whole body.

When he opened them, Bennett's face was inches from his, staring into his eyes. His hips were moving steadily now, thrusts long and deep. Richard pulled him closer for a kiss, and Bennett's movement changed, short, quick stabs that met their target with speed, maintaining an intensity that would drive any man over the edge.

Richard tried to hold back, but he could not. Two days in close quarters with William had left him aching for release, and he was more than ready for it. "That's it," he grunted, letting go, and he felt Bennett flood him with seed a moment later, sending one final, blissful shudder through him, just as it was supposed to be over.

Bennett collapsed on top of him, spent. Richard kissed him passionately, a last nod to their coupling, and then nudged him off his body and onto the bed.

"Thank you," he said. He had planned to be up and dressing moments after they were done, but it was all he could do not to throw a possessive arm around Bennett and fall asleep.

"Thank you?" Bennett asked with a low chuckle, still short of breath. "Have I done you a service?"

"One I sorely needed. You truly were missed."

Bennett turned his head and looked at him, eyes still full of desire. "Stay tonight," he panted, "and in the morning, you may have my arse. You're not the only one who has missed that."

The last time Richard agreed to stay the night, he had lived in the house for eight months before he caught Bennett with one associate and two bawds in their bed. He looked back upon the time they'd spent together then as the best and the worst of his life, but he would not go through it again.

"I can't. My apprentice will worry," he said, grateful for William for the first time since he'd arrived at Bennett's home. Richard had tried not to think of him while he lay beneath his oldest lover, but now, uninvited, William returned to his thoughts.

Bennett left the bed and fetched a rag to clean himself.

"You like him, don't you, this new boy?" he asked as he wiped away the evidence of their intimacy.

There was a question. "I do," Richard confessed to himself as much as to Bennett. "In truth, I like him much more than I should a man I have known two days. He keeps nothing of his feelings to himself. A tender heart and a handsome face are a potent combination."

"There are plenty of handsome faces. I realized far too late that the heart is the key."

Was that an admission?

Richard tucked the moment away in his breast along with all the other little gestures and acknowledgments he'd received that evening.

Finished with the cloth, Bennett tossed it over to him and picked up his discarded clothes.

"How old?"

"Twenty."

"A twenty-year-old apprentice! Well, I suppose I set the precedent when I formed the acting troupe. It's an attractive age, though, isn't it? The charm of youth with the body of a man."

Richard found William charming, but it wasn't his youth he liked. "You know I always preferred older men."

Pulling on his hose, Bennett grinned at him. For once, Richard thought Bennett had earned the right to be a smug bastard about it.

"I know very well what you like, but you've made exceptions before."

Richard could only think of one. "You introduced me to Nick. He had expectations, and I was lonely. That was born of need more than a desire for a young lover."

"I hope the new apprentice serves you better than he did."

That wouldn't be hard. Nick was skilled, but Richard had always wanted more than that in bed. "He was trying to serve me when that brute who came for the money interrupted us."

Bennett's eyes widened, and his smile grew broader still. "Really? You didn't hurry back to him?"

"I promised Geoffrey I wouldn't touch him, and I've already gone back on my word. I don't want to make things any worse."

"But I'm sure your young apprentice has other ideas."

"Lots. And you've seen him. He is almost impossible to say no to."

Bennett looked down at him fondly. "He's lovely, but I've known lovelier, and here you are with me now, instead of at the Spurre sharing his bed."

"Yes."

"I'm at your call every night if you want me," Bennett promised. His voice was gentle, but his face still carried a wolfish grin.

"I might." Richard hoped he sounded casual to Bennett's well-trained ear. He knew already that he would be at the bedroom door come nightfall tomorrow, cursing himself for his weakness and hating Bennett even more. If only Bennett could simply love him or let him go… but none of that would matter when they were in bed again and Richard was moving inside his lover, saving up every signal that seemed to give away what was in Bennett's silent heart.

No one would hurt but him, and Richard could take it when the time came for Bennett to let him down. Even now, he knew he would pay for this later. He always did. Nevertheless, after two years apart, a little heartbreak seemed a small price for a few weeks, maybe even months, of paradise. If he kept his head clear, refused to trust Bennett's words and simply enjoyed them, he might protect himself.

Fully dressed now, Bennett returned to the bed and kissed him again. It was the delicate, gentle kiss Richard should have given William onstage.

William. William will hurt.

Richard pulled away, feeling afresh the burn on his cheek. "I'm famished," he said. "Fetch me something sweet."

Bennett stole another kiss and left without a word.

Flopping back onto the bed, Richard let out a heavy groan. He hadn't asked William for his heart. It couldn't be helped if his was already occupied. Why did he care how William felt anyway? He barely knew him—that was what Bennett would say. But Richard wasn't Bennett, and he hoped he never would be.

Bennett returned, carrying a plate of sweetmeats. "Marchpane," he said. "It always used to be your favorite. Or have your tastes changed over the last two years?"

Richard took a red star-shaped piece from the plate and inspected it. The smell of the sweet almond paste took him back to happier times—and sadder ones too. He took a small bite and found it still delicious.

"No," he said, a hint of regret in his voice. "I've not changed at all."

CHAPTER NINE

WILLIAM WAS still awake when Richard returned, although he was tired. When Geoffrey left, he had stripped naked and climbed beneath the sheets, hoping he would appear enticing. He fantasized a lot about what they might do, wishing for more than the tug he'd got that afternoon. Feeling Richard's hands upon him was wonderful, but he wanted more.

He'd given up on seeing his master again that evening, when Richard walked through the door.

"I worried you would be gone all night," William said, sitting up in the bed, immediately alert. He was so excited that he barely noticed how tired Richard appeared.

Richard went straight to the bed and sat to remove his boots. He glanced at William but didn't seem interested in his body. "Tonight I've returned because I wouldn't have you worry, but I may not sleep here again for a while," he said wearily.

William felt stomach-sick. "Why? Have you been talking to Geoffrey?"

"It's nothing to do with you. I'm working off the debt."

That was a relief. Richard needn't be away every night on Nick's behalf.

"Why should you? Nick ought to repay Bennett, and if he can do nothing but work on his knees or on his back, then let him face the consequences." Richard muttered his disapproval, but William didn't know or care about his predecessor, and he wouldn't be cowed. "He stole from you. He betrayed you. He brought that man here to blackmail you. You owe him nothing."

"William, he was my friend and my lover for two years. I'll not have him in my life after all those crimes against me, but I can't forget our past. I'm not that sort of man."

"That's noble of you. It's a pity he wasn't so loyal."

"I never wanted or needed him to be," Richard snapped, finally finding enough energy to be angry. "I wasn't in love with him, and I don't believe you own a man just because you lie with him. I watched him woo girls often enough, and though I was offended when I discovered he slept with bawds, it is only because I didn't want to be passed the pox. Nick was convenience and friendship for me, and he would have had the money if he told me he needed it."

"So why didn't he?"

This made Richard pause. Eventually he shook his head. "You don't know him. He doesn't work like that."

Richard lay down on the bed fully dressed, and William sank down beneath the sheets next to him. After a few minutes' silence, he found the courage to say, "Now you're back, we should start where we left off."

Rolling over, Richard took his hand and squeezed it. "I'm tired," he said with a yawn. "Maybe tomorrow night."

"You won't be here then. Besides, I need you now. I've been hard half the night thinking about you."

"I'm sorry."

"Please. I was so close before, and I have waited for you. I want you to love me."

"Love you?" Richard gave William the same indulgent smile he had when they were first introduced. "Are you asking for a fuck?"

William grinned at him and Richard laughed. Then he closed his eyes and murmured, "All right."

Shifting forward, William kissed him. Richard opened his mouth a little and let William tentatively probe inside with his tongue. Richard tasted of sweets and good wine. He had said he would be looked after at Bennett's home, and apparently he had not been wrong.

William took the opportunity to explore Richard's body, undressing him slowly as they kissed. When they were both naked, he traced a finger over his lover's jawline, stroking the tidy beard before moving down to his chest, where there was a softer, lighter covering of fine hairs and two perky brown nipples.

He tried to deepen the kiss, but Richard wouldn't let him. "I'm tired," he murmured, but he continued to allow the more delicate pecks, and he pulled William close.

William whipped his hand down now, hoping to persuade Richard's cock he wasn't so weary, but it lay soft against his skin. He pulled his hand away as if burned. "You don't want me anymore." The knowledge was crushing.

Richard opened his eyes but did not look at William. He stared at the ceiling as he said, "It's not that I don't want you. I've tried, haven't I? I can't fuck you because I've nothing left."

"I don't understand."

Richard sat up and pulled William up alongside him. "How do you think I am paying the debt?" he asked irritably.

Of course.

How could William have been so lean-witted as to misunderstand that? Nothing else would be keeping Richard from his own bed every night. "No," he whispered. "Don't sell yourself for Nick."

Richard pointed to his clothes that lay discarded on the floor. "The purse is in amongst that pile there. Count the money. Thirty for Nick's debt, and another five for me."

Five pounds. Was that all Richard Brasyer cost? It was a fortune to William, and yet it seemed like nothing at all. "You're whoring yourself for five pounds?"

Cringing, Richard explained. "It's called patronage. Bennett often supports me through hard times, and I am generous with him in return. Plenty do it."

"Even Geoffrey?"

"No. Not him. And you won't tell him that I've done it either."

"Why not?"

"Because I am ashamed. Now please, let me sleep."

It was a long night. William lay awake wondering what he might be expected to do. It was one thing to pretend to a man like Sam, but another entirely to actually lie with a man like Bennett. On their brief meeting, Bennett had allowed William no dignity, treating him as just another commodity to be bought and sold, and at a far cheaper rate than the gold he was supposed to trade.

Was that how he treated Richard? Richard seemed sure that he would be looked after, but his behavior when Bennett was there didn't suggest any warmth between them.

In the morning, after only a few hours' sleep, William woke to find himself wrapped in Richard's arms, head resting on his chest. Richard was still asleep but had somehow found him during the night, and apparently neither of them minded the position enough for it to wake them. William wondered if Richard dreamed of Nick or Bennett. He doubted Richard thought of him.

Still, it was nice, the comfort and closeness of his body. William had never slept naked until he arrived in Richard's bed, and this was the first time he'd woken in a man's embrace. It didn't entirely make up for the previous night's disappointment, but it was something.

He hadn't woken up excited—it didn't happen every day—but now he felt himself stirring. He tried to will his arousal away by focusing his mind on work, knowing he would get no release for yet another day, but he could not. Eventually, he gave up and simply enjoyed the delicious ache between his legs as he pressed against Richard's body.

Soon Richard awoke. William closed his eyes and feigned sleep, hoping the moment would last a little longer.

"William?" Richard asked, voice drowsy, when he realized what had happened. His grip strengthened just a little, and William was sure he felt a soft kiss on the top of his head before Richard relaxed again. "William, wake up."

William raised his head and smiled contently at him. "A few more minutes, please," he said. "I'm enjoying this."

"If you wish." Richard's hand strayed down to cup one of William's buttocks. "Cupid's arrow must have struck deep. I wouldn't have imagined my presence so welcome after last night."

"I'm not happy you went to his bed, but it couldn't be helped."

Richard winced slightly. "Yes, it's just the way things are."

"I shouldn't have been surprised, anyway. I've been mistaken for a bawd three times since we met."

"You'll get used to it."

William supposed he would, but he didn't have to revel in it. "Am I to get used to it because I'm an actor or because you have a reputation?" he asked wryly.

"Both would be a good starting point. From there you must learn teacher you meet to go fuck his own arse."

The pair of them giggled, and William felt a sublime friction as Richard's body moved against his cock. He shuddered slightly and pulled himself back, breaking the contact.

"Does that thing ever go soft?" Richard asked playfully.

"Not when I'm naked with you." William didn't like to be teased for something he couldn't help, and he had no control over his body's reaction to being in Richard's arms, in his bed. He shifted away fully, sat up, and leaned against the wall behind the bed, pulling the blankets up to hide his stiff prick.

Richard sat up too, taking a similar position next to him, one arm and thigh flush against William's own. "You still want me," he asked seriously, "despite knowing what I did last night?"

The thought alone of what he might have done made William yearn for him all the more. "I've no idea what you did, but I imagine I should like it very much. Perhaps you could show me when your debt is repaid. I will wait for you. I don't care how long it takes."

"You've not the patience for that." Richard continued to smile, but his eyes grew sad. "Besides, I'm not worth it. I'll just let you down again."

"I know you have lain with men before. And I know Bennett was once your master—"

"That does not make it any better. You must forget me, I told you."

"That's what I was trying to do yesterday in this bed. I won't be able to put you from my mind until I know what it is I must forget."

Richard looked him over and then stared into his eyes. "Loyalty is important," he murmured. "I can't give it to you."

"Had I five pounds in my purse, it would not matter what you think about loyalty."

They stared at each other until William could take it no more. "We should dress," he said, moving to leave the bed.

Richard caught his arm. "You understand, don't you? You understand why it is better I do not let myself give in to the urge?"

"Not really, and I do not care to hear your explanation."

William tried to pull away, but the grip around his arm tightened, and Richard would not let go.

"I would have talked of protecting you and of protecting m You are not like other men I have known. We are to softhearted. If you do not wish to hear it, then I will just have to give you what you want, and we must both face the consequences."

William did not believe for a moment he would get what he wanted from Richard. "All I have wanted for days now is to come off," he muttered. "Will you give me the room alone for a while?"

"I'll give you my mouth, and you may do with it as you wish."

There could be no mistaking that. William's breath caught in his throat and his cock twitched. "All the way," he demanded. "You take me all the way to the end, or I'll have none of it. These past few days have been the most frustrating of my life."

Richard responded with a desperate kiss. When he pulled back and looked into William's eyes, he whispered, "I shouldn't do this. I shouldn't."

But he kissed William again, and William realized that whatever Richard's conscience told him, he would do it anyway.

Eventually the kisses moved lower until Richard's head sank down between William's legs. Then warmth and wetness as Richard's mouth closed over the end of his cock.

William gasped and tried to pull back in surprise, but there was nowhere to go. His flesh, already sensitive from being swollen so long, had never known a touch like it. It was the most wonderful thing he'd ever experienced; he knew that, if nothing else. Richard's lips slid down and down, right to the root of him, and it was all William could do not to come off in Richard's mouth after just one suck. He clung to the sensation, struggling not to give in to the ecstasy that was overwhelming him. After so much time spent waiting, aching for Richard, it took the power of every muscle in William's body to hold back.

Mercifully Richard stopped, slowly withdrawing William's prick from his mouth. "You like it?" he asked innocently.

William looked down at him, watched him lick his lips, and felt himself shudder. "I like it all right," he replied. "And though I am trying, I cannot sustain this much longer."

Richard continued to look up at him as he took William's cock in his hand once more. William expected him to suck again, but instead he brought it to his mouth and licked the sensitive tip. That was an entirely new sensation, and a fresh wave of desire washed over William.

"That will not help me hold back," he gasped.

Looking very pleased with himself, Richard asked, "Should I stop?" But his eyes were full of lust, not concern.

"No."

"Then let yourself go. There will be other times."

Richard brought his head back down over William's cock, enveloping him again in moist heat.

William closed his eyes and focused on the sensation. Tight lips gliding up and down, tongue snaking around, licking the head, the slit…. He clung to the feeling for almost a minute, but as it built inside him, he could not hold back, didn't even want to, and he came off quickly, spilling seed into Richard's mouth.

When he opened his eyes, Richard was grinning at him.

"Relieved?" Richard asked. "You've done what you came here to do."

William felt euphoric. His whole body had come alive, and the sensation hadn't fully left him yet. Coming off alone felt good, but coming off with Richard felt like heaven. "Not just relieved," he panted. "I am the happiest I have ever been."

"Good. Have you scratched your itch for me?"

"I think I am more in love with you than ever now," William confessed, regretting it a moment later when Richard nibbled his lip nervously. He didn't want Richard to think what they'd just done was a mistake. "I mean, not in love, but…. You understand what I am saying?"

"I do."

Richard left the bed to dress. His cock was hard, but William didn't press for the opportunity to satisfy him. He didn't want to be rejected and have it spoil the moment. Besides, more than anything right then, he wanted to go back to sleep.

"I must be less forward," William said with a yawn. "I have to keep reminding myself you don't know me the way I know you."

Richard took a seat on the bed next to him as he pulled on his hose. "You still don't know me at all," he said quietly, "but I'm beginning to get used to your ways. It's nice to have some affection. I may have bedded many men, but few have loved me, and even fewer would admit it. Even if you don't truly mean it, it's pleasurable to my ear. I've waited a long time to hear it spoken in earnest."

William's heart leapt. "Does this mean we're lovers now?" he asked hopefully.

"You are still my apprentice, and I am still your master."

"Yes, yes, but when we go to bed—"

"Nothing has changed. You know I will be with someone else tonight. You know I have just used you when I should have left you be."

William remembered all the talk, but he didn't feel used. "If you want to use me, then do it now. You've had nothing from me."

"I've had more than enough from you," Richard said curtly. Then he groaned. "You see, I have hurt you, just as promised. That is the cost of having what you want."

It bruised, but William set his chin, ready to take on any argument Richard threw at him, knowing it would not matter the next time Richard was hot for him. "It was fair bought, and I would do it again. I suspect I will, knowing the strength of your resolve."

Richard shook his head as if exasperated, but a faint smile stole onto his lips as he replied, "No doubt. Now come, we must get breakfast. There's a lot to do this morning."

William sluggishly dragged himself from the bed. Heaven had abandoned him, and it was time to face the world in all its ugliness. He should probably start with the worst of it.

"Before we do anything this morning, I should tell you that I followed that brute last night."

"You did what?"

Richard seemed surprised rather than angry, which was a good sign.

"I disguised myself and followed him. He went to a bookshop on the other side of the river. I don't know the name of the street, but I could take you to it."

"What did he do there?"

"Spoke to the bookseller about you. Well, I think it was about you. They talked as if he'd been to see someone about the purchase of a book."

"A bookseller? You're sure it was that man?"

"I'm positive. He may have paid me no mind, but I had a good look at him and followed him door to door."

William watched Richard turn the information over in his mind. "Will you take me there this afternoon so I can see the place for myself?"

"Of course."

"Good. Now, you must promise me you'll not go sneaking about like that again. It was dangerous and stupid."

William expected nothing less than a telling off, even though he'd done Richard a favor. "Don't worry, I've already had that talk with my cousin," he huffed.

Richard grimaced. "Geoffrey knows?"

"He caught me coming home and saw I'd borrowed a costume from the chest. He wanted to know where you were, so I told him you were with Bennett."

"Lord, he will murder me for this," Richard grumbled, rubbing his temples.

William didn't press for details why, knowing Richard would not give them up so soon, but being a curious person he had to mention it.

"Forgive me if I'm wrong, but I am beginning to think it wouldn't be the first time you've been in trouble."

Richard gave him a sideways glance and half a smile as he replied, "Maybe you are getting to know me after all."

Chapter Ten

RICHARD HAD much to think on as they made their way to the bookshop.

He'd met with the brute earlier in the day and given him the money. Walking away felt strange, but he soon relaxed when he got on stage and saw William. The lad reminded him he would be investigating later. For the first time in a decade, he was eager to engage in spy work. He'd never done it for his own benefit before. Now he understood the use.

He thought too about William, who had surprised him yet again. What was a lad like him doing disguising himself and sneaking around London? His last apprentice had spied on him; had Bennett sent this one to do the same?

He was suspicious for only a moment before he recollected the stuttering, would-be swain he'd met in the village. William was no spy, but spying apparently came naturally to him. Richard would have to watch him around Bennett.

They walked together, but thankfully most people took no notice of them. William dressed in the same clothes he'd worn previously, while Richard disguised himself with a wig and a long cloak. A drizzle of rain allowed him to keep the hood up, and he was grateful for it.

Only one person seemed to recognize them—a street seller, peddling leeks, who called "Hoy!" to William as if he knew him. William ignored the lad and walked on, head down, but he stole a glance back when they were farther up the road.

"You walked a long way," Richard said when he judged them both to be a good distance from the bridge, mindful that it was getting late. He wasn't frightened of being out after dark, but if they were walking into a trap, he would prefer to escape from it in daylight.

"It's not far," William replied. "Just around this corner."

Richard stopped, catching William's arm and pulling him to the side of the road. "That's Fleet Street. Go check it is the right place and then return to me here."

"I don't need to check. I know it's the right place," William huffed. He seemed offended by the suggestion he was wrong. "I may have only been here once, but I took note of my surroundings. I didn't just come to satisfy my own curiosity. I thought it might be important to you."

It was, and Richard was grateful. "In that case, your job is done." His tone was appeasing if not his words. "You may return to the inn, and I will meet you there later."

William grinned mischievously. "I'm not leaving now the interesting bit is about to begin. Anyway, what if you need my help? I didn't bring you here to abandon you."

"And I didn't bring you here to endanger you. Get home while it's still light."

William's eyes narrowed, lips pouting into a sulk. "You cannot make me leave. You owe me the chance to stay and see what's happening. You wouldn't even know about this if I hadn't come here yesterday."

That was true. Richard hated to admit it, but he was impressed with William's courage and ability.

Where did he learn that?

"What exactly were you doing, coming here yesterday? Do you often follow people?"

William turned a faint pink at the suggestion. "Not often, but this isn't the first time. I came to help you, though I must admit I am often curious."

"You are that."

William's blush grew hotter. "I thought I was doing you a favor. I won't bother doing that again."

"You have helped me, and I am grateful." Richard felt a little guilty that he'd not properly acknowledged the value of William's work. "I'll pay you for this information when I get back to the inn this evening, and let me thank you now for what you have done. Now please, you must go."

He expected the lad to march off, annoyed, but William remained. He was defiant and even a little mocking as he asked, "And what will you do? Walk into the shop and demand your money back?"

"I am a touch more subtle than that." Richard felt the sting of William's words. In truth, he hadn't concocted a plan because he was walking into the unknown, but that didn't make him stupid. He thrived in situations that would ruin other men.

"You are their victim, and probably the most recognizable man in London," William argued. "I'm just a customer. I already told the shopkeeper I'll be back today for a chapbook. I can enter unheeded."

That was undeniably useful, but getting inside was the easy bit. William would need a better idea if he wanted a chance to prove himself. Now it was Richard's turn to bite. "So you will go in, buy your book, and leave?" he asked, every bit as scornful as William had been.

William paused. Clearly he'd not thought beyond that.

Richard decided to save his embarrassment. "Listen. If I was to let you in there—and I'm not saying I will—I would need you to look for evidence of who organized this. Check his table; look for papers, receipts, anything that could be connected to me. The bookseller will be the link between our man and whoever ends up with the purse. We just need to find the end of the chain."

"But why use a bookseller as a go-between to collect a gambling debt? It doesn't make any sense."

"That's right, which is our first clue that this is more than it seems. So, who would use it? A bookshop is the sort of place the highest class can frequent as often as they like without raising suspicion. It's a good place to leave a note for someone you don't want to be openly associated with. Men like you might go in for a chapbook or a Bible."

William was still frowning. "You mean men like us?" he asked, sounding slightly affronted.

"Didn't I say that? Not that it matters."

William didn't look convinced but was thankfully willing to let it go. "So you think there's a noble who wants thirty pounds from you?" he asked incredulously. "Seems unlikely."

"It does, doesn't it? The money's unimportant, I think. It's where I got it from that they will be interested in. I'm not convinced I was the target."

They set off again in silence. Richard could see William was determined, but he felt nothing but shame at using the lad for his own ends. It went against his instinct to protect his apprentice, but at the same time, his own interest selfishly pushed him on. He'd told Bennett he wouldn't investigate, but given this information, he must. If Bennett was the target, and it seemed all the more likely given the go-between, Bennett might not be able to trust his men. Richard felt compelled to help him.

The bookshop might even be a dropping point that Bennett used. Richard was aware he visited such places to message other men in their trade. For the most part, Bennett maintained his distance from his associates, but Richard had been a special case when they met, and his celebrity since meant no one batted an eyelid at their association. If Bennett visited him in a rough inn, that meant little to society. Richard was an actor. Where else would they meet?

Richard stopped at the corner and looked onto Fleet Street. William walked on, and Richard was aware this was his last chance to send his apprentice back to the inn.

He never felt good about using men, but he'd done it enough in the past to protect Bennett. They were just men he'd met along the way, most of whom didn't deserve his care. William was different.

Richard had to make a choice—protect the young apprentice he liked so much, or let him go to save the master he'd both loved and loathed over the years. He remembered the pleasure he'd brought the lad that morning, the smile on William's face, the flush on his cheeks, and the warmth he'd felt in his breast in return. He really did like William.

Then he thought of the way Bennett had held him and of the scraps of affection he'd handed out. Last night it had been just enough, but this morning, Richard was less sure when he woke up with William in his arms. Holding the young man felt good physically and spiritually. Better than good, even—although he fought the sensation, it felt right.

As he watched William walk up the street, Richard realized he didn't want to go to Bennett that night. There was someone else he would much rather be with.

But it was too late, he had considered too long, and now he couldn't stop William without drawing attention to them both. Taking up a spot on the corner, he watched and waited while the lad approached the shop.

He would give William a little time to work, but then he was going in after him.

WILLIAM WALKED toward the bookshop without a backward glance to Richard, who he was aware had fallen behind. As he stepped inside and shut the door, he stole a look around and saw his master stood on the corner, watching and waiting.

When he arrived the previous day, he had been nervous, and today was no different. His heart thumped and his stomach clenched into a knot as he stepped inside. Yesterday he had no idea what to expect or what he might do, but today, having half a plan in place seemed to make the task all the more difficult.

He dipped his head politely to the bookseller and went straight to the chapbooks again. He needed to find a way of distracting the shopkeeper so he could search for clues. Before he could light upon an idea, the man was next to him.

"Hollo again, my boy. Can I help?"

William thought on his feet. "I'm looking for a gift for my sweetheart," he said, indicating the books.

"Ah, a girl," the bookseller replied. He was an elderly man and didn't appear in any way threatening. If William hadn't known the company the man kept, he wouldn't have been worried by him at all.

"Yes, that's it, a girl. She's a pretty one," he added hastily.

"I'm sure she is. She must be clever too. Not many girls can read."

William didn't think his heart could pump any faster, but now, having been caught in his lie, he couldn't stop it. Outwardly, however, he maintained absolute calm.

"She is clever, and she'll be able to read perfectly when I've finished teaching her. I thought perhaps you might have a romance or a comedy? Nothing that would shock, but if it put her in the mood to kiss me, I wouldn't be unhappy."

They talked for a while about the different books laid out on the table. William was aware of time passing, yet he made no attempt to search the place. He had no idea how to get rid of the bookseller, who was unlikely to leave the shop floor unattended and step into the back while William was there.

In the end, the solution came to him naturally, as they had discussed every chapbook on display. "Is this all your stock?" he asked. "I'm not sure she would like any of these, but I must get her a gift. Is there nothing more out the back?"

The bookseller looked suspicious and asked, "How much do you have to spend?"

"I've tuppence on me for a pamphlet, no more than that."

"Give me the money."

William handed it over, hoping he could get it back from Richard later, and watched the bookseller go over and lock the door.

Now he felt real panic. "What are you doing?" he demanded, fear in his voice. "Why are you locking me in?"

The old man looked amused. "I don't want you running away with anything while I'm out the back. What do you think I will do?"

"I don't… I'm not sure. I just don't like being locked in."

"And I don't like being robbed. I will be as quick as I can."

The shopkeeper disappeared behind a curtained door, and William listened and waited patiently until he heard him step away from it a minute later and go farther into the back room.

Finally he saw his chance. William hurried silently to the bookseller's worktable, where he found a map of the New World. He lifted it up carefully and underneath discovered a bundle of receipts.

William could only hope what he needed was near the top of the pile. He quickly checked through those near the surface but found nothing. After returning them to the table, he shifted the map and saw a leather-bound notebook full of loose papers, overfull and unfastened. After glancing toward the curtain, behind which he could hear the old man muttering and moving boxes, he quickly reached beneath the map and opened the book. There on top was a sheet of superior-quality paper, folded down the middle. He nudged it open and knew immediately that he had his evidence.

Only two words were written on it—*Spurre Inn*.

Before he could grab the paper, a fist banged on the shop door. William gasped, knowing he had been spotted prying. He spun around to find Richard at the window, still cloaked.

The bookseller snatched back the curtain and started when he saw William stood by the table. William held his breath, but then the shopkeeper saw the hooded figure and narrowed his eyes, muttering blasphemies under his breath.

Approaching the door, he shouted, "Are you a customer or a messenger?"

"Messenger," Richard shouted back in a husky foreign accent, head down so his face couldn't be seen.

"Then come back shortly," the bookseller replied. He turned and left Richard standing in the window.

William chuckled, seeing the bookseller roll his eyes as he walked away.

"He can wait until we're done," the bookseller said. Then he spotted the map William had been looking at.

"That's not a place for a man with a sweetheart," he advised as he walked out the back again.

William looked back to find Richard gone from the window. He quickly lifted the map, grabbed the note, and stuffed it into his doublet before continuing to peruse the Virginia coast until the old man reappeared.

"Here," the man said as he stepped out onto the shop floor with a slim book. "*Venus and Adonis*. Just teach her the filthy bits, or better yet, read her the lot and let her think she must chase you."

William looked the booklet over as if he was genuinely interested before saying, "Thank you. I'll take it."

The bookseller thanked him for his custom, unlocked the door, and let him go.

William had to fight not to run from the building. He walked at a fair pace back toward Richard's corner while his whole body throbbed. This was the same rush he'd experienced when he left the stage after their first kiss—the thrill of having done something forbidden and got away with it. It was exhilarating.

He walked past Richard and continued around to the next street, unsure if he was being followed. He daren't look back and kept moving forward, knowing Richard was behind him, probably holding back to check the same.

William was at the bridge when Richard caught up with him, pulling him into an alley before they crossed.

"You were forever in there," Richard said, voice hushed. "I was worried about you. What was going on? Why was the door locked?"

"He didn't want me stealing anything while he was out the back. He even took my money in case I snuck something while he was gone."

"He sounds a sensible man."

"He was actually quite nice. I feel bad about thieving from him."

Richard's eyes lit up. "You found something?"

William beamed, unable to hide his excitement now. "Here." He pulled the paper from his doublet. "It's not much, but it is proof he's involved as a go-between, just as you suspected. We can watch the building, see who comes and goes." Handing Richard the note, he said, "Look, that's our inn!"

Richard took it from him and opened the paper. His happiness disappeared instantly.

William waited, but Richard did not speak a word of thanks. Beginning to worry, William asked, "Is it not enough? I know we will need to do more work, but I hadn't much time, and it was my first go. Perhaps I should go back tomorrow, tell the bookseller my sweetheart didn't like the book. He might let me change it, and I can look for something else."

Richard continued to ignore him, still staring blankly at the paper.

"Shall I go back tomorrow? Richard?"

His master closed the note carefully and tucked it into his doublet. "You needn't go back. This is all the evidence we need. I know who arranged this."

"How?"

"I know the hand that wrote this note. My God, I know it better than my own."

"Whose is it?"

Richard shook his head. William watched him struggle to get the words out, wishing he could help.

Finally Richard spoke. "I have been set up by the man who paid so generously for my arse last night. This is the work of Bennett Goldfox."

CHAPTER ELEVEN

WILLIAM FROWNED, a mixture of confusion and anger on his face. "I don't understand. Why would Bennett do that to you?"

Richard knew the answer, but he wouldn't share it with William.

"I don't know," he muttered.

"Did he say nothing last night?"

Last night. Lord, how Bennett must have laughed at him when he left. Richard had thrown himself at his former master the way he had as a youth, shamed himself by revealing he was as softhearted and headed as ever, and then promised to come back for more tonight. He would be back, but it would not be for pleasure.

"He said plenty last night, but none of it a clue to this. Let's go back to the inn."

"But—"

"And let's do it in silence."

As they made their way back to the Spurre, Richard imagined everything he might say to Bennett that evening. He was angry, and he would make sure Bennett suffered under the torrent of his rage.

Bennett had lied to and manipulated him in the past, but never did anything as calculated as this. The ruse could only have been designed to win his good favor at a time when they had been apart for so long Richard's feelings might be expected to have cooled. Bennett needed him to be grateful.

Back at the inn, Richard instructed William to change into his own clothes and then fetch the lines from Geoffrey. William did as asked without argument or comment, but Richard could see the concern on his face.

Alone at last, he took up his bag and checked his purse. Fortunately he'd spent nothing of the five pounds Bennett gave him. He had a mind to keep it, given the trouble he'd been caused, but there would be satisfaction in returning it unspent. Besides, Bennett would have got the other thirty back. He might as well have the lot.

William arrived with the script a minute later. He kept his head down, sat at the table dutifully, and didn't try to engage Richard in conversation. Richard was grateful for his silence and that he was not sullen or miserable with it.

Taking a penny from his purse, he went to sit at the table facing William.

"Thank you for your help today," he said as calmly as he could manage. "I'm sorry I was short with you. You risked a lot to get me this information, and I should have shown you my gratitude earlier."

William took his hand tentatively, strengthening his grip when Richard didn't pull away. "I've not finished yet," he said. "I think you need comfort, and I will provide it."

"You have lines to learn." Richard carefully withdrew his hand from William's grasp and stood from the table. "Here is a penny for your dinner when you're done."

William watched him put it on the table but didn't move to pick it up. "What will you be doing?"

Richard could tell from his tone that William had an idea and it didn't please him. "Going to see Bennett."

Eyes narrowing, William set his jaw, determined now. "I'll not let you go," he said. "I've been as patient as I can be with your mood, but this is too much to bear."

Richard was taken aback by his impudence. He'd expected William to moan and sulk but hadn't anticipated demands from his apprentice. "You can't stop me," he replied, too surprised to check William's insolence.

"I can. I get a say in this if nothing else. I risked the noose stealing for you this afternoon."

"And I just thanked you, but that is exactly why I must see him, so you won't have to do it again."

William stood now and placed his hands on the table. He leaned forward. "Don't go to him. He has nothing you could want or need."

It was almost a given that what William desired was behind this, not any respect for what Richard might. "I will not be in his bed again if that is what concerns you. You'll get yours tonight."

"That is not what I'm thinking of."

"I thought you considered naught else, the way you have carried on since we met," Richard retorted. He immediately regretted it.

William's face turned scarlet with fury, and Richard took a step backward. It was unnecessary; William kept himself under control.

"You think I care more about a fuck than I do your life? Or my life, for that matter, if he finds out I'm the one who has implicated him? I don't want you to challenge him. He's rich, powerful—"

"Well connected and influential too," Richard interjected.

"You do not need him to be any more of an enemy than he is. Go to him when you have a clear head so you don't do anything rash."

With anyone else, William would have been right, but Richard was far likelier to regret seeing Bennett when he was calm. That was when he was prone to foolishness. He had forgiven Bennett more than once in the past.

"I do not go to challenge him. I just wish to speak to him for the last time."

"You will achieve nothing by that. You must think sensibly, even though he was your master. You owe him no good-bye."

William was correct, but Richard was not in the mood to listen. If it was to be the end of his acquaintance with Bennett, then he must go. He wanted to see Bennett's face when he realized that, for once, Richard had won.

"You should work while there is daylight," he snapped and turned away from William to signal the conversation was over.

He went to the window and looked out at the fading light, wondering whether he would need a linkboy. Outside he saw the costermonger, the one who'd called to William, look up at him before both their attentions were drawn to an approaching carriage.

It was an impressive coach, even if not a large one. Like Bennett's house, it proudly displayed the wealth of its owner without resorting to size over style. The wood was ornately carved with scenes of foliage and Tudor roses, and it was beautifully painted. A man had to be extremely brave or foolish to visit Southwark with that much pomp—or very well connected with London's underclass.

Richard recognized it instantly, having ridden in it many times. He'd come home in Bennett's sedan chair the previous night, grateful the dark had hidden the gaudy decoration that matched the coach, but the carriage had taken him numerous places over the years. He and Bennett had even shared some good times in it when the velvet curtains were drawn.

"Bennett's carriage is outside," he said as he turned back to William. "You should go downstairs and wait until we're finished."

"What's he doing here?" William sounded worried now, all anger forgotten. "Do you think he knows I took the note?"

"Unlikely. Not an hour has passed since, and it is nothing but a scrap of paper. I doubt it will be missed. Now go."

William didn't move from the table. "I'm not leaving you with him," he said, shaking his head. "No good will come of it."

"He won't hurt me," Richard promised.

"He may not hurt you, but do you trust yourself with him? Honestly?"

Richard had felt certain when Bennett was an hour's walk away. Now he had to admit he was less sure.

"Quickly. Under the bed," he ordered, knowing it was too late to argue anyway. "I suppose it will be easier to keep a clear head with you here listening. You must not make a sound, no matter what you hear, no matter how much it shocks or worries you. If he finds you, then he will make you pay, and the only way I can protect you is to kill him. Don't think I will hesitate to run him through. It will be you or him, and he has lost any loyalty I felt for him."

William disappeared beneath the bed, and Richard arranged the sheets so they fell to the floor.

It seemed to take forever for Bennett to reach the room, and Richard had time to build up the fire while they waited, wondering how things had ever come to this.

When the knock came, he opened the door and let Bennett inside.

"What are you doing here?" he asked gruffly, no more polite than he had been two days earlier.

Bennett was visibly taken aback by the greeting but rallied quickly. Behaving as if Richard had been nothing but polite, he answered, "I was about to return home when it occurred to me that I could collect you and save you the shoe leather."

"I'll not ride with you."

"I thought that was exactly what you planned to do tonight."

"I'll do it, all right, but not with you. Never with you again."

Finally accepting that he could not bluff his way out of this, Bennett frowned. "When you left me last night, I assumed I'd won you back with my generosity, if not my manner."

That was too cruel, even if there was some truth to it. Bennett's words knocked Richard's confidence exactly as he must have intended.

When Richard made no comment, Bennett asked, "No boy today? Or does he approach? Wait, don't tell me. He comes from the rear. Is that what this is about?"

"He is no business of yours, and soon I will not be either."

"Please, just tell me what I have done now," Bennett said wearily, taking a seat on the bed. It creaked, and Richard could only pray William was all right beneath it.

"You know what you have done. You just do not wish to give yourself away if I am annoyed at you over something trivial. You set me up, sent a man to this very room to extort money you knew I didn't have so I would be forced to come to you."

"Where did you get that idea?"

"I did a little investigating."

Bennett raised an eyebrow. "After you swore not to? You couldn't help yourself, could you? Spying has got into your blood."

"I hope you're enjoying mocking me. It will be the last chance you get, so make the most of it."

Bennett appeared perfectly relaxed now the truth was out, not taking the words as any threat to his well-being. "I did not intend to hurt you, and if I have, I apologize unreservedly. To wound you was never my intention, and it pains me to hear you suffer. I needed you to trust me again, and it seemed the quickest way."

Richard couldn't help himself and laughed bitterly at the absurdity of the situation. "You wanted me to trust you, so you lied to me? No, you didn't want my trust. You wanted my service in your bed. You made me your fool yet again, and I let you."

"It was not like that. I deceived you, yes, but I have need of you for a job, and I knew you would refuse if I didn't give you a reason."

"Spy work? You did this because you wanted me to spy on someone?"

"Why else?"

Richard felt an all-too-familiar swell of emotion—disappointment mixed with grief. On the numerous occasions Bennett let him down, he always felt a crushing weight on his chest and a sickness in his stomach. Today was no different.

"How can you be so cold?" Richard asked, struggling to keep his voice steady. "In the sixteen years I have loved you, all you have done is use me. Every time I have been seduced by your lies into forgiving you, and all you've ever wanted was a body to fuck occasionally and someone to protect you when you needed it."

"No. That is not true," Bennett murmured. "You swore to protect me, and I have taken advantage of that, but I didn't ever lie to you in bed. You know how I feel about you."

"You're right. You've never made me promises or told me you love me. There's no lie there."

Bennett flinched. "Listen to me—"

"No. Never again."

"Please. I need your help."

Richard knew that. Bennett wouldn't be bothering with him at all right now if he didn't.

"Ask someone else. I can't be the only man you've strung along."

"There's been no one else for years, and you know it." Bennett was speaking quickly now, and sweat was beginning to form on his brow. "I'm sorry my lie offends you, but I had to win you over. I have no hope without you. My life is at stake, and you are the only person I can trust."

In spite of himself, Richard listened. "Who wants you dead?"

Bennett shook his head. "We can't talk here. Come to my home."

"So you can lie to me and fuck me again? Never. Get out of here."

"Please. I will die if you don't help me."

"I don't believe you. Go."

"One last time!" Bennett barked, and Richard was stunned into silence.

In all their years, all their disagreements, Bennett had never shown desperation before. Richard always believed it beneath him. To see him that way now was disconcerting.

Richard took a deep breath. He forced calm into his voice. "I was twenty-one years old the first time I heard you say that, and I have heard it many times over the years. Now here you are, asking for help again. Why should I believe it now?"

"This time it is true meant." Bennett was calmer too, but the tension in him was still obvious as he sat hunched on the bed.

"I'm not sure I've ever had the truth from you. You can't convince me of it now."

Bennett closed his eyes and pursed his lips. When he opened them, he said, "If you will not trust me, then please trust that you'll be rewarded so generously you need never work again."

As ever, Bennett thought his endless supply of gold would buy him whatever he desired. Richard didn't want a penny of it. "Keep your coin. In fact, I have five pounds to return to you. I assume you'll get the rest back from your henchman later."

He held out the purse, but Bennett wouldn't take it.

"I told you that money was a gift, and I intend you to keep it no matter what happens. I did not buy your company last night. You gave me that for free, and that five pounds was my gift in return. Keep it now. I want you to remember that I always helped you, even when you didn't need it."

"I will remember you only as the man who made me a thief and a liar, and worse besides. I will not be in your bed or your employ again, I promise you that."

Bennett's face flickered for a moment, and Richard thought he saw a grimace of pain. It was gone before he could be sure.

Bennett collected himself. "Don't be so quick to refuse. You might need me again one day."

Richard's nose wrinkled in disgust. "I'd rather starve than go back to you."

"Would your men?"

Caught off guard by the question, Richard had no answer to that. Bennett had paid their wages more times than he cared to admit. Their relationship had always been about more than just the two of them.

Bennett rose and walked toward him slowly, as if Richard were an animal he did not wish to scare. "I can provide you right now with four new plays and the costumes required. Call them a gift to the company. I have no use of them, but your men might. Come to my home now, and you can bring them back here tonight."

Richard knew he should say no, but new material would be most welcome, and the costumes would be worth a fortune. With so many purses to fill, it was hard to turn down the offer. Even Geoffrey would take it.

"I'll accept your gift, but I make no promise," he relented, hating himself for his weakness, but if he did not take the costumes, he would regret it later. He could always use something to sell to pay the men during the lean times.

Bennett gave him a relieved smile, which faltered when he apparently realized Richard hadn't forgiven him. "Thank you," he said quietly. "That you'll even consider this gives me hope."

For the first time in years, Richard didn't care how Bennett felt. He was more worried about what was going through William's mind as he lay on the dusty floor. It surely could not be good.

UNDER THE bed, William kept his breathing as shallow as possible and lay so stiff his body ached. Although he felt the pain, it didn't bother him. His discomfort was mitigated by fear. If Bennett discovered him, he would suffer more than the embarrassment of having been caught eavesdropping.

To calm his nerves, he focused on the conversation instead. That didn't help. When he'd slipped beneath the bed, he trusted Richard with his life and his love. What an ass he'd been to do that!

He could no longer ignore the situation he was in, and for the first time, he admitted to himself that he did not know Richard at all. He'd left everything he knew and cared about because he wanted a tumble with a complete stranger. Lying on the floor listening to them, he felt a bigger fool than Richard was professing to be.

But William didn't think Richard a fool and wouldn't have described him as such. Right then, if someone asked, William would tell them Richard Brasyer was a dangerous man to associate with, and he was a liar.

Finally he acknowledged the most damning fact of all. He could have put up with all of it if he still had a shot at Richard's heart. Now he was sure he had no chance of that.

"Come," Bennett said. "Let's away and fetch your trunk of things for the company. We can discuss the job at my home."

Richard sounded hesitant as he replied, "Not yet. My apprentice will worry about me. I'll leave when I am finished with him."

"Finished?"

"I wouldn't want to go to you as needy as I did last night. I'm not about to make that mistake again."

"Later, then," Bennett replied.

William heard Richard let him out of the room.

Door shut, Richard came straight to the bed and loudly whispered, "Wait."

William heard him walk to the window, where he remained for a few minutes. He guessed Richard was watching the carriage to make sure Bennett was gone.

A short while later, he returned to the bed and peeked below it. "You can come out now."

William crawled from underneath, covered in dust.

"Well?" Richard asked, nervous. "I'm sure you have something to say."

William couldn't look at him as he brushed his clothes down and readied himself to leave. While he collected his few possessions, he muttered, "I have risked myself three times for you, and you didn't deserve it. I only have myself to blame for that. I'll go now."

He had no idea where he was going. He didn't even care if he ended up dead in a ditch. He simply had to get away if he wanted to maintain any dignity.

Richard silently watched him snatch up his things and toss them in his bag. William was out of the inn and marching down the shadowy street when he next heard Richard's voice.

"William! Stop!" he shouted, chasing him up the road.

Ignoring him, William walked on. Suddenly, Richard grabbed him, manhandling him into a tight alley between two buildings.

"Don't go," Richard growled low in his ear. "I'll not let you leave like this."

William struggled, but Richard held him firm and stared into his eyes. As William wrestled against Richard's grip, he knew he should be frightened, but he was not.

"Get off me," he hissed, "or I will scream for help."

"That will guarantee men keep their distance," Richard whispered back.

His face was faintly lit by the glow of firelight from the windows on the main street, and William could see he wore a pained expression. He wasn't angry and didn't appear to be a physical threat, despite his tight hold.

William stilled, and Richard's grip relaxed a little, though Richard swiftly pressed his body against him instead, pinning him to the wall. He was ashamed to find being this close to Richard was still arousing. Apparently learning the truth about his master hadn't changed how his cock felt about him.

"You have lied to me and used me," he said, ignoring his lengthening prick. "How can you expect me to stay after that?"

Richard looked away from him, shaking his head as if to clear it. "I don't expect you to stay. I want you to, but I have earned no loyalty from you." He stepped back and released William, standing aside so he could pass. "Get away from me while you can, and don't look back."

William had been determined moments before, but now he couldn't bring himself to walk away. He remembered Geoffrey's words that, given his past, if Richard truly cared for him, he would let him go.

Now he really was a fool, but Richard was a hard habit to break. "I have to know everything. All about your past and what I am likely to expect in the future."

"No. It's too dangerous for you to stay here. The more you know, the greater your risk."

"It's too late for that."

Richard leaned back against the wall next to him. "Lord, I have been stupid and selfish," he groaned. "A broken heart would have been better than the danger I've put you in. I should have thrown you out the moment I saw Bennett at the inn."

"You didn't, so here we are, and now you owe me an explanation."

"I was a spy. There's nothing more to say than that. I'm sorry I made you one too."

"I enjoyed spying, and I don't hold you responsible for my involvement in it, but you should have told me your history before I stepped into the bookshop this afternoon. That would have been fair, even if it wouldn't have stopped me."

Staring at the ground, Richard shook his head miserably. "You profess to love everything that is distasteful about my life except the secrets I tried to protect you from. I cannot believe you would still be here now if you knew the true extent of my past. Tonight you heard the word *spy* for the first time and you turned tail. There's worse than that."

Of course there was. "You can't have committed a bigger crime than loving Bennett."

Richard closed his eyes and tipped his head back against the wall. "I have regretted my association with him many times but never as much as I do now. I'm sorry, for you, and for myself, that I ever met him. He has led me to places I can't come back from, no matter how hard I have tried."

"Enough of your self-pity," William spat. "I don't care what you've done for a coin, or a thrill, or to keep yourself alive for another day. I don't judge you for any of that."

Slowly, Richard straightened up and turned to look at William through narrowed eyes. "You will regret it if you don't," he threatened. "I'm not some hero in a play. I'm the dangerous bastard you'll be stuck with if you stay."

He was good, but William could see the gesture was contrived. This was clearly Richard's last attempt at scaring him back to Oxford.

"You will have to train me to be an equally dangerous bastard and have done with it," he muttered.

Richard relaxed his menacing look, but he didn't smile. "So you are staying?"

"For the moment."

"That shouldn't please me. But it does."

"Don't flatter me," William snapped. It would have been a treat to hear yesterday, but today it was distasteful.

"I didn't say it to charm you, even if it seems that way now. I like you, William. You may hate me for my secrets, but that is the only thing I wish I had told you before."

"You could have done if you hadn't been so busy in Bennett's bed."

William's cock still stood stubbornly tall, although the contact between them was long since broken. This was all the proof he needed that he was not, and had never been, in love with Richard. Right then, he didn't even like him, but he still desperately wanted to fuck him. Richard had made him feel alive in bed that morning, and he needed more.

He peeled himself off the wall and stood in front of Richard. "I offered you comfort, and I meant it," he said. "Let's go back to the inn."

"No," Richard mumbled, head down again, pathetic. "You needn't force yourself for me. I didn't deserve you when you wanted me, and I deserve you even less now."

"My feelings for you have not changed. Even now I long for you to have me."

Richard looked up at him, dim light reflecting in his eyes, face only half-illuminated. The dark alley was a world away from the stage where he'd first delighted William. He was no longer dazzling, but the man whom William had longed to kiss remained.

"I'm cunt-drunk," William continued. "That's what my brother would call it if you were a woman."

Richard reached out and took his hand, then pulled him gently until William leaned lightly against his body.

Their lips touched.

It was a delicate thing at first. William liked being kissed passionately on the stage and in bed, but there was something to be said for this treatment too. He could better appreciate the soft yielding of Richard's mouth as it opened for him, the tickle of his beard, and the confidence of his tongue.

Soon the kiss deepened, and Richard's hands moved to his head, long fingers trailing through his hair, before gliding down his back and cupping his arse.

William craved that more than anything. He'd been so focused on the needs of his cock and balls that he'd let his arse go unregarded those first few times, but he wanted Richard inside him more than anything and was not afraid for his first time. He knew well what to expect, well enough to know he wouldn't be getting it here in the alley.

Richard continued to explore William's body, hands pushing into the back of his hose, finger burrowing down the cleft of his arse, just as it had the day before, lightly brushing his hole again. William shuddered, grateful he'd found a lover as keen as he was for that. Perhaps Richard would even like William to plough his arse in return. That would be a thrill.

But William's real desire right then was to make Richard come off by any means he could. He fumbled his way into Richard's hose and found his cock to be just as hard as his own. For a moment, he was nervous, and his touch was light because of it, but Richard huskily ordered, "You know what to do. Don't hold back."

So he didn't, but when a hand found his own cock, he did try to match Richard's pace. William's release would be all the sweeter if they could both come off together.

They kissed right up until the end, when William needed his breath more than ever. He'd not done it standing up before, and his legs ached from the exertion of just holding up his body. He had to cling to Richard for support and lean against his shoulder even while they tugged each other. His lover didn't seem to mind, and William felt one strong arm clutch his waist tightly while the other pumped his cock.

Then he was gasping, shaking, and Richard was whispering unintelligible promises in his ear as they both spilled their seed onto the cobbled street.

Richard continued to hold him up while he regained his composure. William was grateful for the care and the release, until he saw Richard lick his hand clean. Then he wanted to begin all over again.

Lifting his own hand, he looked into Richard's eyes and tasted his seed. It was thick, salty, a little bitter at first, mellowing into sweetness as he held it on his tongue. He'd never tasted his own and didn't know what to expect, but he wanted more. This was the very essence of his lover, and he would take it a hundred times over even the most honeyed treat.

Richard swallowed heavily at the sight, his breath still coming deep. "Do you like it?" he asked gruffly.

"Bennett is waiting," William said, ignoring the question. He had to be all business now if he wanted to be taken seriously as a spy.

They tucked themselves back in. Richard tried to kiss him again, but William pushed him gently away. "We've an appointment to keep."

"Yes, I must go."

"*We* must go. I'm your apprentice, and he wants to discuss a job. He should expect me to be there."

"I hate to refuse you now, but we are playing his game still. You can come to help me carry the costumes back, but Bennett won't speak of spy work in front of you."

That was more than William had been expecting. Now he had a foot inside Bennett's home, and he would take it. From there he could find a way to listen to their discussion. Unable to trust Richard anywhere but the bedroom, he would have to rely on his wits if he wanted to know what sort of situation he found himself in.

Chapter Twelve

It was full dark when they arrived at Bennett's home, but, as ever, the house was brightly lit.

Richard expected William to make a comment on the property, but if he was impressed, he did not show it. His expression was worryingly determined for a man who'd come only to help carry a box.

Richard approached the house with a bellyful of nerves on the lad's behalf. William seemed intent upon ruining himself, and Richard hadn't the will to stop him. Protecting him hadn't worked, and releasing him only tested Richard's own resolve, and found it wanting. What more was he to do?

What a question to ignore! He knew exactly what he should do—apprentice William to another master. Better still, it should be with another company. Geoffrey was adamant from the start that the opportunity shouldn't be wasted, and William had shown onstage how much he deserved the position. He should continue to train, but with a man more suited to tutoring. A man without a past.

Perhaps Richard could sweeten the deal for all parties by continuing to offer William a bed for the night. But would that be safe? Probably not.

He had one other option, and he now selfishly scrabbled at it. William was intelligent and capable, he'd gained in confidence quickly, and he was brave. He wanted to be a spy. Perhaps he could be taught how to protect himself too.

They stopped at the front door, but Richard didn't knock, not yet. William stood next to him, silently waiting.

When William gave him a questioning look, Richard whispered, "Dull your wit." Then he knocked.

The door was answered by the same servant he'd met the night before, who appeared surprised Richard had arrived with a guest. He led them through to the well-stocked library and immediately left to fetch the master of the house.

Richard watched William, who had been unmoved by the outside of the property, widen his eyes as he looked around the room.

"Impressed?"

"Now I know what you see in him," he said.

That hurt. He had hoped William thought better of him than that. "You think I loved him for his money?"

"No, although that would not put anyone off. Look at all these books. There are more in this room than I saw in that bookshop yesterday. Where I come from, you're educated if you have a Bible in the home. He must be well learned. Pity he has never been taught manners."

The door opened, and Bennett stepped in. He was fully dressed this time, but his doublet was not fastened all the way and his shirt billowed out the top. It was obvious he'd readied himself in a hurry. His manner was easy, however, likely because he knew he had no one to impress.

Ignoring Richard, he looked to William. "Hollo again, good man. I wasn't expecting you this evening."

William bowed his head deferentially. "My master said there might be a load to carry, sir. I've come to help."

"At this time of night? You could have waited until the morning."

"I wouldn't let my master make two trips."

Bennett laughed merrily, as if their last encounter had never happened. "You wouldn't let him?" he teased. "Who is the master here?"

Richard barely felt the insult. He was too angry at Bennett to care what he thought. "You are," he replied, but there was no respect in it. "Now, we must talk business."

"But you have brought your apprentice. Tarry awhile. Let him enjoy the surroundings."

Bennett turned his attention back to William, who was no longer bowing his head. His expression was neutral, but Richard knew the contempt he would be feeling.

Grinning at William, Bennett continued, "Tell me, boy, what sort of things has Richard been instructing you in?"

"Acting, mostly."

"There's no better tutor for that. Anything more practical?"

William feigned ignorance. "In what sense?"

"Oh, I don't know... swordplay, perhaps."

A devilish smile found its way to William's lips. "Forgive me, sir, but I ask again, in what sense?"

"He likes to play, this one, doesn't he?" Bennett said to Richard, but he didn't take his eyes from William. Dipping his voice only slightly, he told William, "Crossing swords is fine sport however you do it, but Richard must be careful that you do not stick yours in him while you practice. Leave that to us fighting men. If you come at him untrained with such a weapon, he may get hurt."

William's smile disappeared. "Quite correct, sir," he said with a distaste he didn't bother to hide. "Only the most inept fool would injure him somewhere important. After all, he only has one heart."

"Enough, both of you!" Richard barked. Bennett scowled, and Richard promised, "I'll punish him for his impudence later."

Bennett looked back at William, who met his eyes bravely. They stared at each other until Bennett composed himself and returned to his usual, genial self.

"Why punish him?" he asked, as if he were above such things. "I assume he learnt it apprenticing to you. Shall we go talk somewhere he won't be forced to listen?"

"I want to see the plays and costumes first."

"As you wish. Come with me. The boy can stay here."

Richard followed Bennett out of the library and across the hall into the opposite room. Outwardly it was used for storage, but Richard remembered the secret passageway it contained. From there you could spy on any room in the house.

A chest blocked the hidden door. Bennett carefully opened its lid and leaned it against the wall.

"Four plays—" He pulled bundles of paper from the top. "—and all the costumes required for them."

The clothes were mostly new and finely made. There were several elegant dresses and suits, accompanied by matching shoes and hats. Even the servant's garb was well done, and it appeared otherwise authentic.

Richard dug through until his hand touched soft velvet. He pulled it out and found a whole bolt of the material in a deep plum color. "Purple velvet?" he said, dropping it abruptly. "You know we cannot wear this, even on stage."

"Then give it to your boy to make an undergarment for himself, if it's not beneath him."

"Where did you get it?"

"I couldn't possibly reveal the name of my client."

Richard knew all too well whom Bennett worked for. Richard had performed for the Queen more times than he dared to count, and he knew how seriously she took her fragile position. Purple was for royalty alone, and on even the lowliest actor playing the grandest Queen, it would not be tolerated.

"I'm not taking it, but we will have the rest if I agree to the terms."

"You may have these things even if you don't. I've no use for pretty dresses and prettier words."

Bennett removed the velvet, returned the scripts, and shut the chest. Seating himself atop it, he said, "The job is a simple one. It has come to my attention that my name is on a list. I want you to confirm that and make a copy."

"Where?"

"Cambridge."

"Cambridge!" Richard did not fancy that journey any more than the work when he got there. "It will take four days to get there and back, and that's without the time spent doing the job. What is the company supposed to do while I'm gone?"

Bennett shrugged. "They've lived without you before."

"We are only just back in London. I can't leave now. Half the audience comes to see me, not the play." It sounded vain, but it was true. Richard understood his own value to the company.

Bennett crossed his arms and stared at the floor. "I will reimburse them for any lost takings and do whatever else may be required for you to accept. I will even say please. This is personally important to me, and I won't trust anyone else with the job."

"More likely no one else is stupid enough to take it," Richard snorted.

"I have asked no one but you. You understand the importance and the urgency."

"I do not, but I am sure you will tell me."

"I'll speak no more until you agree."

Richard eyed Bennett warily. He didn't want to trust him, but he could see the fear Bennett was fighting to conceal. Richard had sworn to protect him many years ago when he received Bennett's ring, and though he hated him now, he couldn't bring himself to refuse.

"Damn you, Bennett," he muttered.

Bennett rose and hugged him. "Thank you," he said, visibly relieved.

Richard shrugged him off. "Don't thank me yet. You must pay me well, or I'll not do it. And not just the clothes and the scripts. I want money too."

"You shall have plenty of that, before and after the job is complete."

"Be as generous as you like, because this is the last time I ever help you. After this, you may ask no more."

"I swear it."

A dull thud outside the door drew their attention. Richard's breath caught, and he was unable to move. Bennett hurried to open it, but before he could touch the handle, Richard blurted, "Stay back! I've got my dagger. I'll go."

It bought whoever was outside only a few seconds, but Richard hoped it was long enough. He yanked open the door and found the corridor empty.

Bennett pushed past him and stalked across to the library. There he found William lounging in a chair, feet up on the table, reading a book. William jumped up as if caught when they entered, and he dipped his head submissively.

"Were you in the hallway?" Bennett asked him, his tone icy.

"Were you in the bedchamber?" William shot back, raising his chin.

Richard hated to admit it, but playing the jealous lover was a smart move. What a pity William had to rely on it after revealing that he'd been listening in.

"This is Master Goldfox's home, and you will respect him in it," Richard growled at William, playing along. "No matter your feelings for me or how you have seen me talk to him, I will not put up with a surly apprentice. We will discuss your behavior on the way home. Now come, help me with the load."

"Wait!" Bennett roared before they could leave. "I've had no answer. Were you in the hallway?"

William bit his lip. "Yes," he admitted, averting his eyes with a show of fearful respect.

"What were you doing?"

"Looking for a servant to sneak me something from the kitchen. I was in need of a little comfort, knowing my master had gone off with you again. Then I stumbled, and heard you both in that room, so I panicked and ran. Please forgive me."

Bennett looked him over carefully as if still deciding whether or not to trust him. "You're a willful boy, aren't you," he mused.

"Not normally, sir. I'm concerned for my master, that's all."

"As am I. I'm worried you'll do him more harm than good with your disrespect and ill humor."

Appearing suitably cowed, William squeezed his eyes tight shut and said, "I apologize."

"Thank you. You may go wait outside in the carriage. I'll have some of the servants bring the trunk."

William bowed respectfully and left. Richard almost believed it was more than an act, but despite their short time together, he knew the lad better than that. He wondered what Bennett thought.

"At least he's loyal," Bennett said, turning back to Richard.

"Yes."

"And really very lovely to look upon. But you get to do more than just look."

When Richard made no comment, Bennett asked, "Will you tell me his name?"

Bennett would already know it, but Richard indulged him. "William Moodie. Not that it will do you any good, as there's nothing to know about him. I will give you now, for free, all the intelligence you may gather. He's the most uninteresting young man you'll ever meet. He comes from a village so small it is not even on the map, and a family of yeoman farmers that are of no consequence to anyone."

"Perfect! Would he be available to work?"

The offer was no less than Richard expected. "When would he find time to work for you? He has a job."

"So did Nick, but he never turned down the chance to make a shilling on the side."

"A shilling for his arse? At those rates, I'm not surprised."

Bennett seemed surprised—insulted even—by the suggestion. "I have never paid for Nick's company. He was always for you alone. Someone to give you comfort when I could not."

"Someone who would never fall in love with me."

"And someone you would never fall in love with. I've seen what happens when you are shown a little affection. You snatch for it."

Richard had heard enough, and if Bennett carried on, he would walk away from the job. "I'm leaving. Meet me at the Spurre tomorrow morning. Have the money and the details ready for me."

He let himself out and went to the carriage, where William waited. He climbed up next to William and put his arm around him for comfort.

"Not a word until we get home," Richard whispered to him.

William nodded silently.

A few minutes later, two servants arrived with the trunk. It was loaded onto the carriage, and then a third stepped up carrying a basket with two stoneware flasks, an assortment of foods, and a small box.

Bennett followed. "For your journey," he said as the servants handed them the basket. "Some warm spiced wine, two slices of game pie, bread, boiled eggs, roast venison, and the last of the marchpane."

Richard was hungry, so he took the provisions. "Thank you. William?"

"Thank you, sir," William said, head down.

"Enjoy them," Bennett replied. "I will see you both on the morrow."

They journeyed in silence back to the inn, mindful that the carriage driver would be listening in.

ARRIVING BACK in their room, they found the fire had not yet burned low, and the space was warm and well lit. William slung back the lid of the trunk and pulled out the plays. Then he started to look through the clothes.

"These must have been expensive."

Richard had taken a seat on a stool by the fire and was watching him, noting William's curiosity about everything. Dresses and doublets, shoes and hose, William looked over each one, but he didn't care for the finer details.

"Bennett has a particular talent for spending money," Richard replied. "Surely you noticed?"

William put the clothes back and shut the chest. "The only thing I noticed was what an arrogant prick he is."

"He's a rich and powerful man, and you are the youngest son of a yeoman farmer, apprenticed to me, an actor, which is only marginally more respectable than being a prostitute. Bennett can say what he likes to you and get away with it. You have to accept that."

"But you are so rude to him," William argued. "Am I not to follow your lead?"

"You must show absolute respect, just as you would to any person of a higher rank than yourself. He and I have known each other a long time, and my tongue runs freer than it should because of that. He barely tolerates it from me. He won't take it from anyone else."

William took a stool and sat next to Richard. "I think it's time you told me your history with him," he said seriously. "I told you I'll only stay if I know everything."

"That's a longer story than we have time for tonight, but I promise you I will tell it when I return."

William huffed, so Richard repeated, "I promise."

"Why don't you tell me what you're doing while you're away? That can't take too long."

"You couldn't hear us through the door?" William smiled slyly, and despite himself, Richard grinned back. The young man's pluck continued to impress him. "Tell me what you heard," he pressed.

"Not much. You're to go to Cambridge to copy some list or other. After that, I heard nothing."

"Because we heard you."

Even in the firelight, Richard could see William was embarrassed.

"I should have been more careful. I was crouching down, trying to see through the crack at the bottom, and I tumbled over. I won't do that again."

"You won't be spying again. This time next week, I will have done with it for good."

"Tell me you haven't said that before."

"I can't. But this time I have you to think of. I won't help him again."

William rose from the stool and fetched the basket of provisions Bennett had given them. They'd eaten the savory food during the journey, but the sweets remained. He pulled out the box of marchpane and brought it to Richard.

"May I have a piece?" he asked, though it was clear he intended to whether or not Richard allowed it.

"You may eat the whole box if you wish. Like it or not, this job will fill my purse, and then I can fill your belly with as many treats as you like."

William took one and nibbled a little of the edge before taking a larger bite. "It's delicious," he said around the mouthful.

The scent of almonds filled the air, and Richard found himself reaching for one too. They ate in silence for a time, slowly savoring the sweets.

William put the box away before Richard could take a second.

"Save some for tomorrow," he said. "We'll want it after the long walk."

Better to get this over with now than in the morning.

"You're not coming," Richard told him gently, mindful he should break the news with care.

William must have anticipated this, because he took the refusal in good humor. "It's too late," he said simply. "I'm already involved."

"You're not."

"I'm your apprentice, remember?"

"On the stage alone. I won't let you be a part of this."

William left the table and went to undress for bed. He appeared perfectly relaxed as he stripped naked and disappeared beneath the sheets.

"William? You are listening to me, aren't you? You're not coming."

"I heard you."

Richard was sure he'd heard, but it was clear he hadn't listened. "So why aren't you sulking? I thought you wanted to come along."

"I do, and you won't be able to stop me."

Richard went to the bed and quickly undressed too. William lay watching him, with a smug smile on his face.

"This is exactly why you're not coming," Richard said as he slipped under the sheets with him. "You're giving all your secrets away. You've given me time to prepare and all the proof I need to explain why your presence would endanger me."

That had him. William rolled over, turning his back to Richard. "I told you, I must know everything," he said sullenly. "I presumed you'd want the same honesty from me. If you want to pretend I would give information away, so be it."

"Trust me, the only thing I want is to close the door on this part of my life. When that is done, you may hear every detail of my past and say whatever you wish. I look forward to it."

William rolled over and stared at him. He pouted slightly, and Richard longed to kiss him again, but he held back. Let the lad come to him.

William didn't, just watched Richard and waited. When nothing was forthcoming, William abandoned the subtle seduction and went for the kill instead.

"You want me to trust you, but you lie to me," he muttered. "You're no better than Bennett."

That wasn't fair. "You can trust me to always have your best interests at heart. I'm not like him."

"You lived in his secret world. You're no different at all."

The bed was in a darker corner of the room, but there was enough light from the fire to see William's eyes; Richard dragged his own gaze from the tempting lips and tried to see the truth in them. William had the same determination he'd seen earlier that evening.

"This won't work," Richard said. "You can't guilt me into bringing you along."

William let out a small grunt of annoyance and then tried what Richard hoped was his final tactic. "Has today meant nothing to you at all?"

William shouldn't have described himself as "cunt-drunk" if he wanted Richard to believe he was in love with him now. It seemed William had worked out exactly what Richard meant to him at the same time Richard had begun to realize the strength of his own feelings. "It did," he admitted, "and that is the main reason why you're not to be involved."

William turned away again, and the conversation was over.

CHAPTER THIRTEEN

IT WAS dawn, and William sat in Geoffrey's room. Richard had woken him in the dark, and with the warning that Bennett would arrive before sunrise, he'd ushered William out to knock on Geoffrey's door. The sun was now up, so William guessed an hour had passed. Still, Bennett had not come, and William had long since overstayed his welcome in his cousin's bedroom. Luckily, Geoffrey's apprentice had stayed out all night, and William was able to creep underneath the empty blankets on the pallet. Neither of them slept again, but it gave William time to think about what he was going to do.

Eventually Geoffrey dragged himself out of bed and over to the fire. "Come on," he said through a yawn. "Get up and tell me what's going on."

William followed. Sitting down by the low fire, he said, "Bennett is coming. He will bring instructions for Richard, who will then be on his way to—"

"Don't tell me!" Geoffrey said. "I don't need that sort of detail. Am I right in thinking Richard has agreed to do some spy work for Bennett Goldfox?"

"That's correct. He has received part payment by way of a trunk full of costumes and four new plays."

Geoffrey's eyes widened. "That is only part payment? Must be a big job."

William made no comment. He had no idea how big a job it might be. It sounded easy enough, but he'd come to realize nothing in Richard's life was simple.

The noise of a carriage outside drew their attention.

"There he is," Geoffrey muttered, "the devil himself."

They stood at the window and watched Bennett leave the coach and enter the inn. William went to the door and listened, waiting to hear Bennett walk by in the corridor.

"Come away from there," Geoffrey hissed, pulling him back. "You'll do yourself no favors by learning too much."

"I don't care," William whispered back, returning to the wood and pressing his ear to it.

"Richard won't thank you."

"This isn't about him."

"Then why put yourself in danger?"

"Because I like it. It's exciting."

Geoffrey was stunned into silence. Then he waved his hand as if he was done with him and walked away.

William shut his eyes so he could hear better. After a moment, there was a shuffle of feet and a knock on the next door. Bennett had arrived.

RICHARD SAT by the fire awaiting Bennett.

They hadn't arranged a time, but he considered Bennett to be late. He didn't want to waste half the morning waiting for him when he could be on the road to Cambridge, and his former master knew that. As time passed, he began to worry. Perhaps this had come too late to save Bennett from whatever threatened him.

Eventually, the carriage appeared, allaying his fears. Bennett knocked on his door a few minutes later and was let in to find him packed and ready to go.

Bennett looked around the room and checked under the bed. "No William this morning?" he asked casually, sitting himself down on top of it.

"He's with Geoffrey in the next room."

"I suspect that is for the best, but I hoped to see him before I leave."

"His manners won't be much improved. Please do not trouble yourself with him."

Bennett seemed amused by the comment. He was his usual easy self, despite what had passed between them the previous evening.

"To business. You'll find all the details you need within this letter." He removed a packet from his cloak.

"Very good, but I am still waiting for the accompanying payment."

"Here. Twenty sovereigns." Bennett handed him the letter before removing a heavy-looking purse from his belt. "You'll have a hundred more when the work is done."

Richard took the bag and weighed it in his hand. He looked inside and found it was mostly smaller coins, which would be easier to divide up. Between that and the five pounds he'd had the other night, he was a wealthy man again.

Most of it would have to stay with Geoffrey while he worked, but that would be no problem. Richard knew he could trust him.

"Thank you," he said, not bothering to count it. "Anything else I should know?"

"There's a good horse for you outside. It's a hunter from my stable, and I'll want it back when you're done."

Richard looked out the window and saw a tall brown beast stood next to Bennett's litter. It must have been extremely well trained if he wanted it back. Bennett wasn't a man to worry about the money it cost or care for the animal. Richard was about to refuse, when he saw it was fitted with a threadbare old blanket for a saddle and reins that looked tired. The horse wouldn't draw too much attention, and it would shorten the journey. He nodded his acceptance.

"That's it, then," Richard said. "Ask your man to stable the horse before you leave. I must say good-bye to William and arrange for his keep before I go."

Bennett stood and walked to the door, where he paused. "I suspect you will be gone before I will. You've a long journey ahead, and I'm going downstairs to have some breakfast in the bar now. You may join me before you leave."

"You're not seeing William again if that's what you're thinking," Richard muttered, ignoring the offer. "You can't buy him with a good breakfast and a small purse."

"I don't intend to buy him. I just want to make peace, and I will do it even without your permission. You will be away for weeks or more. Wouldn't you rather I met him now with you than alone later?"

Richard's heartbeat quickened in fear at the idea of William being alone with Bennett. He narrowed his eyes and threatened, "If I return and find you have been anywhere near him while I'm gone,

I will walk all the way back to Cambridge and tell whoever you are spying on what you've done. Do you understand?"

Bennett inclined his head in acceptance. "Very well. My offer of breakfast still stands. Say good-bye to your boy first." He left, and Richard took a seat at the table, where he began to divide up the money. He was interrupted moments later by Geoffrey, who walked straight in without knocking.

"Is he gone?" Geoffrey asked, his tone short.

These were the first words Geoffrey had spoken to him in two days. Richard had worked through silent glares the previous day, and he was unsure whether this was an improvement. He was glad of it, nevertheless, as he would need Geoffrey's help.

"Only downstairs for his breakfast. Where's William?"

"He's supposed to be in my room right now, but I suspect he snuck out the moment I left. He didn't put up a fight when I told him to remain. He says you're off again."

Richard wondered how much information William had passed on to his cousin. "Just a short while," he said casually. "A week or two at most."

He indicated the money on the table, and Geoffrey eyed it distrustfully and said, "He also said you were paid in plays and costumes."

"That chest over there. Take a look."

Richard continued to bag up the money while Geoffrey looked through the costumes.

When he turned back to Richard, his tone was conciliatory. "You didn't have to do this. I know times are tough right now, but we would have got by."

"There are a hundred pounds at least in that box, two hundred, probably. We've pawned a lot of our good stuff. How could I turn this down?"

"Things are looking up." Geoffrey shrugged, giving the worst performance of his life. "We're back in London."

"Until the plague levels get too high again. That might be next year or next week. This gives us a bit of security."

Geoffrey took a seat at the table and looked at the money. "What about all that?"

"It's my personal payment. My loyalty to Bennett is gone, but he's bought himself a favor. Look after it for me. If I don't return before the year is up, use it to buy William a share in the business."

Geoffrey balked at the idea. "He's only been apprenticed to you a few days, and this is an awful lot of money. Are you sure you want to do this? Don't you have family to leave it to?"

"I'll be back," Richard replied, ignoring Geoffrey's words. He would rather not discuss his family, and it wasn't like they needed the funds. "This should be easy money I'm earning. I tell you this only if I take sick or fall from my horse. I don't want to leave you encumbered by your cousin. Train him up, teach him a bit of responsibility, and then let him play the lead where he can. He's handsome, and that will draw a crowd if nothing else."

He picked up one bag with three sovereigns inside and handed it to Geoffrey. "You must look after all the rest, but this one is a gift for you. Spend it or keep it, it's yours now."

Geoffrey peeked inside the purse and closed it back up.

"Thank you, but I shouldn't accept this, not knowing how it was obtained. I believed you when you said you were done with all that. You promised you weren't going to see Bennett again."

Richard wondered which time Geoffrey referred too. He had promised it often enough over the years.

"Once you're in, you can never truly get out, but this is absolutely the last time. I've more to think of than myself now."

"You have. I would never have brought William if I'd known."

"I know. But I'm grateful you did."

Geoffrey had relented, but he didn't look like he believed Richard at all. "So you have decided you fancy him?" he asked, referring to William.

"I fancied him from the moment I saw him." Richard smiled for the first time that morning at the memory.

Geoffrey rolled his eyes, but he was smiling too. "I understand. We Moodies are handsome men. Some might even say irresistible."

William certainly was. "Would you be angry if I told you that I'm falling in love with him?"

"No, not angry," Geoffrey replied, with grudging acceptance. Then he softened and said, "You're still risking your life for the last man you loved. You'd better do the same for him."

Even after days of conflict, Richard was reminded why Geoffrey had been his best friend for so many years. He felt himself beaming, despite the situation.

"Thank you. It means a lot to know I have your blessing."

"It didn't stop you when you didn't have it," Geoffrey snorted. "But I'm pleased to give it now. Just don't go telling him right away. He will follow you to the gates of hell if he believes he has your heart."

"I think that's his plan regardless."

Shaking his head wearily, Geoffrey said, "I don't know what to do with him. He seems to think sneaking around is a grand adventure."

"You once felt the same."

"Not for long, but it was fun while it lasted."

Richard was mindful that he needed to be on the road soon and didn't have time to reminisce. "This brings me to the second thing I need from you. You must leave William locked in here, just for today. Don't even let him go to the theater."

"My pleasure. I don't want him running off any more than you do."

"Thank you. I know it means more work for the company—"

"We're going to need a different play today!" Geoffrey gasped in realization, practically jumping up off the stool. "I better go sort things out."

He made for the door before returning for the purses. "Best not leave these lying about," he said. "I suspect there's more here than we'll take at the theater the whole time you're gone."

"Lock them up with my savings," Richard instructed, "and send William back in here if he's not run off."

When Geoffrey left, Richard collected his things and took up his sword and dagger. He hoped he would not need them; he generally used them just for decorating his person, but he knew how to wield both. Bennett had seen to that training and given him the opportunity to use them in combat.

William entered a few minutes later, looking pleased with himself. It was a stark contrast to the previous night and indeed that morning. Richard didn't trust his mood.

"Hollo," Richard said, standing to greet him. "You seem happy this morning."

"Why shouldn't I?"

"I'm going away. Won't you miss me?"

"Not a bit," William replied with a smirk.

Richard knew he should be wary of William's intentions, but he couldn't resist his good mood. Allowing himself the pleasure of playful teasing, he said, "I thought you were cunt-drunk. Have you sobered up?"

William looked into his eyes and breathed. "You're as intoxicating as ever."

One of them was still love-sotted, but Richard knew it wasn't William. Still, he could not hide his delight at the words, even if they were meaningless. "Come here," he murmured. "Kiss me so I may leave you tipsy, and you will not be able to follow."

William went to him, and they embraced. His lips brushed Richard's only briefly before he pulled back. "Take me with you, and there will be more tonight," he promised.

"There's none of that on the road." Richard drew back abruptly. He had bargained for affection too often in his past to enjoy it now. But despite himself, he nearly gave in. Resolve abandoned him when William was around, but danger strengthened his will. He had to get away from William for both their sakes. "I should go." He collected his things together and slung the bag on his back. "Geoffrey will provide your board while I'm gone. There's some spending money here for you too."

He pressed five shillings into the lad's hand. It would buy him a very good time if he chose to remain in London. Richard hoped it was incentive enough for him to stay.

William looked at the coins and then tucked them into his purse. "Thank you."

Richard kissed him again and pulled him close enough that he could feel William's cock hardening through their clothes. His body responded in kind, and his heart with relief. There was a comfort in knowing he owned that part of William, even if he didn't have his love.

"I will miss you," Richard said.

Then he was gone, out the door before William could even say good-bye. In the corridor, he hesitated only a moment before putting the key in the hole. His lover would be angry, but he would be alive too. That was the most important thing.

He locked William in.

Richard hurried downstairs, not inclined to stick around and hear William's protest. Stepping into the bar, he found Bennett seated at a table with a large breakfast spread in front of him.

"Richard!" Bennett called as Richard walked through the door. "Come and eat."

He was hungry, but he wasn't going to waste time with Bennett. He wandered over to examine the fare, and when he was close enough, said, "Thank you, but I must get on the road. I've a long journey. I'll just take some of this with me."

He helped himself to a loaf of bread and some slabs of roasted meat, stealing some bites as he loaded the food into his bag. Bennett caught his eye, his expression betraying a hint of nerves.

"Is this all safe to eat?" Richard asked, pausing midchew. "I know you were expecting William."

"I would not poison your boy," Bennett replied, but he looked away uneasily. "I think he might be too useful for that."

"He won't spy for you. Especially not if I'm the target."

Bennett cast his eyes about the room. No one was paying them any attention. There were too many voices chattering for anyone to be aware of their conversation.

Appearing satisfied, he replied, "A pity. Your boy gave me the impression he might be quite good at it."

Richard reached into his bag to find the two flasks they'd been given the previous evening and filled them both from the ale jug. Then he took a seat next to Bennett, though he didn't intend to stay. He had only one thing to say, but he would do Bennett the courtesy of saying it discreetly.

Leaning closer, his voice low, Richard said, "William will have no time for spying, but he will likely be good at a lot of things I'm going to teach him. I'll fill him up with my knowledge, and he will do the same for me in return. That will be a joy in itself, but what makes me happiest is that I will never need your mastering again, no matter how many years we are apart. And we will be apart. There is no room for you anymore."

Richard took a sip of his ale and tried to enjoy the discomfort on Bennett's face. He was disappointed to find he could not. He'd hoped for anger or even petulance from Bennett. Instead, for the first time, he saw Bennett truly unmanned.

Bennett shook his head as if to clear it. Then he looked Richard in the eye. Voice strained, he said, "I didn't come here to confess, but I may as well if your intention is to cut me from your life for good. I thought much upon your words last night. My feelings have perhaps not been clear, or maybe they were too clear when you were young and I didn't have the same regard for you as I do now. I didn't know when you were eighteen what you would be like at twenty-five, or thirty, or today. You are the one regret in my life. I wish I had loved you better."

It was too late. Richard could not believe it now. "Loving me at all would have been a start."

Bennett appeared pained. "I'm sorry I hurt you."

"I already agreed to take the job and took your coin. You needn't keep up the pretense. I don't work for crumbs of affection anymore."

"This is no charade. I cared for you when you were young, but I have been deeply in love with you these last nine years."

Abruptly Richard rose from the table, legs knocking the edge in his haste. His heart thumped, and he felt sick with anger. Of all the lies Bennett ever told him, this one hurt the most. "This would have worked two nights ago, but not now and never again," he hissed. "And you can find another man to go to Cambridge. I am sick of being your fool."

Bennett remained in his seat. He stared at the table while he calmly said, "Please, Richard. Hate me all you like, if that is what you think I deserve, but you must do this job. There is no one else I can ask. I don't care if you empty my pockets, you must do it."

Before Richard could refuse, Bennett looked up and said, "Here's your apprentice. Maybe he will have something to say."

Chapter Fourteen

Five minutes earlier

RICHARD'S KEY rattled in the door, and William immediately went to work.

He'd turned over Geoffrey's room searching for the spare key, but hadn't found it. He did, however, discover a spectacular ballock dagger, its gold hilt encrusted with jewels and the scabbard decorated with a delicate filigree. Thinking it might prove useful, William slipped it into the back of his hose and covered the handle with his shirt.

Now he threw it into his bag and gathered up everything else he owned before sitting down at the table to check through his purse. He had the five shillings Richard gave him, plus another five he'd brought from home, which was a lifetime's savings. He judged it was more than enough to get him to Cambridge. Finally, he hurried to the window. Too far to jump, but he had another idea.

He opened it and was relieved to see Sam already in his usual position. "Oi, Sam!" he shouted down to him as if they were friends. "Have you still got that penny?"

The street seller appeared thrilled to see him. "For you? Any day!" he called back.

"I'm trapped in here. Help me down."

Sam crossed the road to the inn and put down his basket. He turned over a large empty beer barrel that stood outside and climbed on top. "Hang out the window, and you should be able to reach my shoulders."

A few people stopped to look at what they were doing, and William hesitated. He didn't want to end up being accused of thieving, particularly not with Geoffrey's dagger in his bag, but he had no other choice.

"Come on," Sam said. "I've got you."

"Is there a fire?" one of the bystanders shouted up to William.

"No," William called back as he climbed out the window. "My master locked me in."

"Who's that?"

"Richard Brasyer."

There was a ripple of laughter, and William reddened. For the first time since he'd arrived in London, he felt ashamed of what he was.

His feet touched Sam's shoulders, and he let go of the window ledge, immediately bringing his hands to the wall to take his weight as he crouched down. His helper swayed beneath him slightly but remained upright, and soon William was clambering down his body and they were both jumping off the barrel.

Show over, the bystanders walked away. Sam picked up his basket again.

"Thank you," William said. "I owe you a big favor."

Sam shrugged. "So you're an actor?"

"Yes. That's why I was in the dress. I play the girls."

"I'm not getting that suck, am I?"

"Not today, but you can have my name if you still want it. I'm William."

"Not today? That's a promise for later," Sam said with a wink and a smile.

William made no actual promises but thanked him gratefully again before he said good-bye. They could be friends, if nothing else. Both were chancers and obviously had more in common than that.

He turned his attention back to the matter at hand.

Bennett's carriage remained outside, and, having no idea which way Richard would have gone, William decided to go speak to him. He would hold his tongue, even bow and scrape if he must. If he could just find out where Richard would be staying the night, then he could make his way there and meet with him. By then it would be too late for him to return to London, and Richard would be forced to take him along.

Stepping inside, he looked around for Bennett and found his table. William was shocked to see Richard was still with him. He tried to step back outside, but it was too late. Bennett had already spotted him by the door and was waving him over. A moment later, Richard was looking at him too, his face twisted in anger.

William shrunk back against the wall. Even when Richard had believed William stole from him, he hadn't reacted like that.

"Come here, boy!" Bennett called to him merrily, as though totally oblivious to Richard's displeasure. "Your breakfast is getting cold."

William approached slowly, head down. He knew Richard would be annoyed when he turned up unannounced, but he hadn't imagined this. He expected his master to lash out, but when he arrived at the table and looked into Richard's eyes, the rage appeared to be under control. William saw nothing but unshed tears.

"What are you doing here?" Richard asked. His manner was stiff, but William was no longer worried.

"I'm coming with you."

"Then come with me upstairs. The job has been canceled."

William was unsure whether or not this was a trick to lock him up again, but he could do nothing but follow.

Then Bennett stood, drawing their attention, and bowed deferentially as he indicated an empty stool.

William knew he was being mocked. "I thank you, sir, but I must go with my master."

"He can wait a moment while you dine."

"Thank you again, sir, but I am not hungry enough to eat."

Bennett sat and their eyes met. The man's gaze narrowed, just for a moment, before he relaxed back into his usual easy manner. "Please, allow me the pleasure of your company."

William didn't know how to refuse without being openly rude again, so he sat. Richard stepped around behind him and put a strong, possessive hand on his shoulder. Immediately, William felt comforted and thankful too that Richard's ill temper was not because of him. He didn't seem to be able to escape his desire for Richard's good favor any more than he could escape his desire for his kisses, his hands, and his mouth.

"I have a gift for you," Bennett said amiably. "Richard forgot to take it last night."

William thought quickly. It had to be the purple velvet he'd heard them discuss. "Forgot?" he asked carefully. "I know he refused some fabric you offered, but when we checked the trunk, nothing else seemed to have been forgotten." Richard's hand gripped his shoulder, so William added, "He told me himself when we were in our bed last night. He said you offered it to me for underwear, but that he prefers me not to wear anything at all."

Bennett's smirk turned to a snarl. "Richard, how does your apprentice know the details of our private conversation?"

"He asked me about the costumes, so I told him. He knows nothing more than that," Richard replied.

William kept his eyes on Bennett, but he thought Richard sounded convincing enough.

"I see." Bennett helped himself to a slice of meat from the table, tearing off a piece and popping it in his mouth. William watched him eat leisurely, wishing he would be dismissed. When Bennett had eaten his morsel and wiped his mouth, he shouted, "Watch! We need the watch in here! There's a thief!"

The drinkers fell silent and turned around to look at them.

"What are you doing?" Richard growled.

As ever, Bennett was unperturbed. He pointed at William and loudly declared, "This boy has attempted to steal my most precious possession from me."

"Don't do this," Richard said, pleading now.

Bennett shook his head. "He must be punished for what he has done. But don't worry, I intend to be lenient. Whipping will do for me. If I can persuade them not to hang him."

William was numb, realizing too late that he should have stayed in the bedroom and waited. Better yet, he should have stayed in the village. This wasn't the romantic adventure he'd anticipated.

He felt Richard's hand on his arm and stumbled backward as Richard dragged him from his seat and toward the door.

"Come with me. Now!" Richard ordered.

William was pulled back into the moment. They ran and stopped abruptly outside the inn, where a horse waited. Richard snatched the reins from a startled footman's hand and clambered up onto its back.

He held out a hand to William. "Get up behind me now!"

William scrambled up and wrapped his arms around Richard, who kicked the horse a second later. Then they were off at a pace, tearing through the streets while people leaped out of the way. He could hear Sam calling to him amid the commotion, but he couldn't speak to reply.

Much to William's surprise, Richard was an accomplished rider and steered them safely through at speed, shouting apologies to people as he passed near them but keeping his eyes on the road ahead.

William clung tightly to his waist and gripped the horse with his thighs. He daren't look back, instead keeping his head down, face buried in Richard's shoulder.

They seemed to be riding through the streets forever, but it could only have been minutes before they were in the countryside. William had no idea where they were, but he knew they'd not crossed the bridge so could not be on their way to Cambridge.

They came to a stop in the fields outside the city. When William didn't relax his hold on him, Richard said, "You're safe, I promise. No one is following us."

William let go and slid off the horse, exhausted. He looked back down the road, and Richard was right—no one had come after them.

William slumped down to the ground, tired and miserable, but mostly frightened still. Burying his face in his hands, he babbled, "I don't understand what is happening. I don't understand why he would lie like that when he knows it could get me killed."

Richard climbed from the horse and crouched down next to him. "Here," he said softly as he reached into his bag. "I got some of that breakfast before I fell out with Bennett. Have a little—it will make you feel better."

"Thank you."

William took the food, though he wasn't hungry at all. He nibbled at a piece of bread and drank a flask of ale in silence while Richard read through some papers.

When Richard looked up again, he appeared troubled.

"What is it?" William was unsure he actually wanted to hear the answer.

Richard held up some papers but didn't pass them to him. "You're getting what you want. We're going to Cambridge."

"You said the job was off."

"It's back on again now. I know Bennett, and this will all go away if I can get a copy of this list."

Richard found the other flask in his bag and took a drink. He seemed so normal again, yet he'd risked his own life to save a man he'd met only days before. Some of the luster he had on the stage was back.

"Thank you for rescuing me," William offered, full of regret for his choices. "I'm sorry I didn't stay in the room. I've been so stupid."

Richard reached across and took his hand. "There's nothing you could have done. Bennett would have found another way to get to you if it hadn't been this. It is my fault. My loose tongue has been the problem right from the start."

They both blamed themselves, as if the man behind all their troubles had done nothing wrong. William might have been stupid, and Richard had his past, but Bennett was the one who'd tried to ruin him.

"Why would he accuse me of theft? Was that about the bookseller's note?"

"Unlikely, even if he does know you took it. He did it to punish us both, and to force me into doing his dirty work."

"Like we'll do it now," William scoffed.

Richard let go of his hand and got up off the ground. Brushing himself down, he said, "You know a little of what is going on, and that makes you a threat to him. You can join Bennett, or you're against him. We've got no choice now."

"But why didn't he just ask me?"

"He doesn't care what you think about it. Everything he does, every word, or look, or gesture, is part of the game to him, and we are just the pieces he plays with. He knew he would win. Even if you agreed, I would not have done, but he must have known I would take you with me if I had to. This is probably what he's wanted all along."

"He's not controlling us. What if you'd left me behind?"

"That was never going to happen."

William dragged himself up and dusted his clothes down. Now the shock was wearing off, he was raging at the injustice of it. "I'll not work for him," he spat. "He'll not have his way now."

Richard stared at the ground, slowly shaking his head. William guessed he had said that himself often enough.

"You've no choice. Bennett always gets what he wants by any means necessary. He already has you."

"But we do have a choice. We just don't do the job. Let's disappear for a few weeks, come back, and tell him we've done it. He can relax for now and suffer the consequences later."

It seemed a reasonable enough proposition to William, but Richard continued to shake his head. "I'm angry at him—probably angrier than you are right now—but I'll stab him in the heart myself before I let someone else get him in the back. Anyone bringing him down could easily take others with him."

"Don't talk to me about anger. That whoreson has accused me of theft, not you. He has put a death sentence on my head, not yours," William bit back furiously.

Richard snatched the horse's reins and held the animal tight. "Easy," he said quietly, "easy," though the horse was unruffled.

William knew it was for his benefit rather than for the horse.

"Only he can remove the charge," Richard continued. "Don't you think that's a good reason to keep him alive?"

He was right, of course. "I think that's the only good reason," William relented.

"Come on," Richard said wearily. "Let's see if we can find a raft that will take the horse across the river. If not, we'll be in for an even longer ride."

He helped William up onto the hunter and climbed up behind him. "Take the reins. I will show you what to do. Hunters don't ride like your farm mares."

William felt the heat of his savior's body at his back, and for a moment, things didn't seem so bleak. He wasn't alone. He was with Richard, the man who could make him do anything. The man who, it seemed, would do anything for him in return.

Richard wrapped his arms around William, then closed his hands over William's as he held the thin leather reins.

William leaned back against Richard and tilted his head to the right. Richard seemed to understand the invitation and left a soft kiss on his neck.

"I will get you out of this mess," Richard murmured against his skin. "You need never fear while you're with me."

William didn't reply, but he was glad to have heard it.

CHAPTER FIFTEEN

EVEN WITH two riders, the horse could move at a fair pace. They trotted to the riverbank, and Richard managed to find a raft to take them across the Thames. He noted it was a brave beast, a little nervous of the uneven keel but not skittish. No wonder Bennett wanted it back.

They had time to catch up, and so rode at a comfortable pace for several hours before they could stop and rest the animal again. Mostly they were silent. William seemed lost in his own thoughts, and Richard let him be. William had to be frightened and confused by the morning's events. Undoubtedly the lad was brave—*foolhardy* might have been a better description—but he could not have anticipated Bennett would make a false accusation against him. Richard wished he'd warned William that his former master did not fight fairly.

He also wished he'd shown more restraint when dealing with Bennett. How could he expect William not to behave the same? Now William had paid for it with a charge of theft, and Richard knew what being beholden to Bennett truly meant. This was the first time Bennett had resorted to fear to get what he wanted from Richard, and Richard could not hope it would be the last.

Occasionally his thoughts drifted back to Bennett's admission. *Love* wasn't a word that had ever been in Bennett's vocabulary, even during the times Richard had been almost sure Bennett felt it. He'd laughed when, as a mere stripling, Richard said it to him. That was another mistake Richard had made more than once.

Feeling rage well up in him, he focused instead on the task at hand.

The instructions were vague. A list was to be found in Trinity College, kept in the private rooms of a fellow of the college named Jacob Hobbes. There was no note of his background or what he taught, and nothing about the purpose of the list they sought to copy.

Bennett did include a paper with details of their associates he knew to be in Cambridge at present. Richard scanned it, aware some were friendlier than others, and was happy enough with the information. Now he could be sure whom he needed to avoid.

They were nearing Cheshunt, a small settlement at roughly the halfway point on their day's journey, and he gently pulled the horse to a stop outside the village.

"I'll get us a late lunch and some ales," he said to William. "You take care of the horse and then come join me inside."

Soon they were eating bowls of pottage and big hunks of dark bread. It was good, better than the food at the Spurre, and cheaper.

William had got his appetite back and gulped the food down. He was talking again too, chattering in a lively manner with the saucy serving wench who fetched their drinks and casually discussing the stage with Richard.

Richard wondered if William was as keen to get back to it as he was. "You seem in good spirits, considering your situation," he noted when there was a brief lull in the conversation.

William shrugged, his mouth full of the soupy stew. He swallowed and said, "I did a lot of thinking as we rode. My life may well be quite a bit shorter that I assumed it would be. I'm going to take what comes to me while I can and enjoy it."

Richard smiled at him. He was impressed by William's resilience, which was far greater than his had been at that age. He also wondered exactly what William meant by "what comes to me" and, most importantly, whether the strumpet was involved.

"So you play with girls too?" he asked. He hoped he sounded lighthearted. Richard didn't mind if William liked both men and women—many of his previous lovers did, and he knew that was natural enough—but the lad was making him possessive, and seeing William play with someone else provoked a jealousy he was ashamed of.

William let him suffer a moment, then replied with a wink, "Only for sport."

They returned to the road, Richard leading the horse and William walking beside him. They would be on the stage now if they were in London, and William hummed some of the music played during the performance the day before.

"Missing your skirts?" Richard asked.

William gave him a lopsided grin. "Not the costume, no. I'm just wondering what they're doing now we've abandoned them."

"They will be fine. The company has coped with much worse."

William nodded, though Richard knew he had no idea what that might be.

"What must Geoffrey think?" William asked.

"He will be cursing you, me, and Bennett too, probably."

"I did not want to make him angry," William murmured.

"I promise you, however angry he is when we return, it is only to hide his worry. You're his family. He cares about you."

Richard looked around. The road was busy, but there was no one close enough to hear them or notice much. He snatched up William's hand, quickly kissed the knuckles, and dropped it again. That bought him a smile, and when their eyes met once more, he saw a hunger in the lad. Unfortunately this was not the time or the place to satisfy it.

"Don't dwell on life in London," he said, "neither your worries nor the pleasures. All your focus right now should be on staying safe until this job is over."

William snorted quietly. "Is that actually possible when you're spying?"

For some men, whose luck seemed limitless, but it was much harder for others. However, carelessness and bad luck generally went hand in hand.

Richard thought of the thud outside the door in Bennett's house the previous evening. "Yes and no. Perhaps it is better if you are not involved."

"But you said Bennett wanted me."

"He does, but it's likely he just wants you to spy on me in the long run, not anyone else. I can do this alone. There is no reason to put you at risk."

"The biggest risk to me is if you fail, because I will have no one to help me when I have to do it for myself. Let me try. I'm getting used to being in charge of my own destiny, and I don't want to give that up for good because of him."

"All right," Richard agreed, knowing that feeling well enough. "But if I feel you're not ready, then I won't let you go into the college. I'll not lose you to save Bennett."

"So the list is in a college?" William asked casually, ignoring the warning entirely.

Curiosity lit up his eyes. William may have realized the danger, but given fresh details, his interest still piqued. His love for adventure had been wounded, but it wasn't yet dead.

"Yes, Trinity, in fact."

"Never heard of it. What's on this list anyway?"

"Names. I've no idea of the purpose."

They walked on together for a while in silence. Eventually, William said, "You promised to tell me your past."

"I did." And there was no getting out of it now.

"Go on, then. How did you get into this business?"

That was a question Richard had asked himself many times over the years, and he never came up with a satisfactory answer.

"I've known Bennett since I was eighteen. He was a family friend, schooled alongside my older brother, John. When our father died, John bought me an apprenticeship in his workroom."

"As a goldsmith? That must have been expensive."

"It cost my entire inheritance. My father loved me, but I was the second son, and a wayward one at that. My brother had no idea of Bennett's other profession, but I've always suspected he knew of his proclivities and put me there because he knew mine. Whatever the case, it was a good investment for the shame of the family. I trained for a year, but it can be delicate work, and I do not have gentle hands."

"I like them well enough," William interjected, giving him a wink.

"If only I had been your apprentice. Bennett was rarely there to see my progress, and he ignored his workmaster's concerns. He had other things on his mind, and my brother was his friend. I think he believed I just needed time."

Bennett had been unusually lenient, doubly so because Richard had not yet made known his desire for his master. Richard just knew that on the odd occasions Bennett visited the workshop, his heart beat with an intensity he'd never known. Better still, when Bennett looked at him, his whole body came to life. Something in him believed Bennett could sense it too. Perhaps that was why he'd been allowed to stay for so long.

"I was there a year before he was persuaded that I would not do. He called me to his home and offered me a new position spying for him. I accepted instantly, glad to get out of the workroom and into something that would pay handsomely and allow me to travel. He set up the playing company, Goldfox's Men, to be my cover, and for two years I did many a job for him while the troupe played."

"Why did it end?"

Richard bit his lip. Thirteen years had passed, yet he still felt the pain of it acutely. "The death of an enemy," he murmured. "I loved spying when there seemed to be no consequences. That taught me it was not a game."

William looked horrified. "You killed a man?" he whispered, looking around to make sure no one would hear.

It was a long time ago, and Richard had done what he had to do. He didn't expect William to understand. "I defended myself," he said simply. "One of us had to die that day. I'm not ashamed of winning a fair fight against a man who wanted me dead, but I knew I didn't want to be in that position again."

"So Bennett let you go?"

"I made myself useless. It didn't last. I was almost twenty-one when I left his employ, and I'm thirty-four now. He always knew what to say to draw me back. Just as surely, he let me down afterward. I never learned."

William looked down at the road. They walked for another minute before he asked, "Have you always been his lover? I can see no other reason for your loyalty to him."

"Bennett comes and goes in my bed, always has. We were last together two years ago but fell out when the plague drove the company out of London. He asked me to choose between him and my men. There was no contest. No matter how much I cared for him, I couldn't abandon them when they needed me the most. It was not the first time we argued. I've known him sixteen years, after all."

"A lifetime."

"It has felt like it on occasion. He took my virginity the night he recruited me as a spy. I think he only held back before for the sake of my brother. When he decided he could do nothing respectable with me, he did what he liked."

"And you let him?"

"I wanted him to."

William scrunched up his nose in distaste. "How can you love him? He may be handsome, but I think he's one of the most repulsive people I've ever met."

Richard couldn't disagree with that. "I don't love him," he muttered. "Not anymore."

"But you did, and for a long time too, I'd wager."

"I was young enough, and stupid enough, to think myself in love with a man I barely knew. When I realized he was trouble, I was young enough, and stupid enough, not to care. Sound familiar?"

William's face flushed, and Richard wished he hadn't said it, but he couldn't take it back.

"Actually, I've been thinking about that, and you were right," William mumbled, eyes on the road ahead.

"About what?"

"I'm not in love with you."

It was nothing Richard didn't already know, and nothing he wouldn't have encouraged, but he didn't like to hear it now his own heart was committed. "A pity," he said softly, not bothering to hide the disappointment in his voice. "I was beginning to quite enjoy your tender heart."

William looked across at him, chewing his lip. Richard would have given anything to kiss him again right then.

"You shall have to enjoy me in other ways," William said.

That was something, but it would have to wait. "I told you, there's none of that on the road."

"Why not?"

"It's bad luck."

"Is that all? When I left my village, I decided I would make my own luck," William retorted, a little more confident again.

He probably thought highly of his success in getting to London and securing a place in Richard's bed. It would be fair to point out that William's luck had apprenticed him to a spy, made him a criminal, and put a false charge on his head, but Richard wouldn't do it. The lad had hurt him, but Richard had no desire to wound him in return by listing his failings.

"Your luck has run out," he said gently. "And mine has been gone for years. I'll enjoy you all night long when we are safely tucked into bed together back in London, but I do not indulge myself when there is spy work to be done. Things went wrong the last time I tried it. That was the day my rival ended up dead."

"There is all the proof I need that my luck is gone," William huffed. "Another week without coming off will be pure torture."

It was long past nightfall when they reached Bishop's Stortford and stopped for the day. Richard managed to secure private quarters at an inn, and they both ate good suppers before retiring to their room. Richard declined a pallet for William, pretending he could not afford the extra farthing, and they slipped into bed together gratefully.

Richard had no idea how much time passed, but despite the long and tiring day traveling, he could not sleep. William apparently felt the same.

They lay still and silent. Richard wondered if the lad waited for him to nod off so he might satisfy himself. He tried to guess whom William would think about and hoped it would be him, even if William now realized he'd never truly been in love with Richard.

Reminding himself of the confession brought him down a little, but it was for the best. No good would come from a love affair between them. And he'd only just met William, so it didn't tear into him the way Bennett's earlier declaration of love had; it merely bruised. In a few weeks, when the shine wore off and William was just another handsome youth he knew, he might feel better, but it was probably too late for that. Richard anticipated that the bruise would only grow bigger and ache harder. He had fallen in love quickly, something that had only ever happened once before in his life, when he was eighteen. That had lasted sixteen years. If Richard lived sixteen more, he doubted he would ever love another man again.

He concentrated on William's physical attributes instead in an attempt to lift his mood and give him pleasant dreams.

William's body was perfect, muscular but not bulky, obviously built by hard work on the farm and a healthy diet. His arse was well rounded, his cock long, and thick, and delicious. His face was handsome, his manner pleasing, but his passion for Richard was what had really made Richard fall for the lad. After two years of bedding none but Nick, William made him feel desirable again, and more than that. For the first time in his life, Richard felt lovable.

Despite all, it wasn't that which had captured his heart. Richard had begun to fall in love with William in bed the previous morning, but watching him walk into the unknown that afternoon truly won him over. Here was a man who could potentially understand and even embrace all parts of Richard's life. Even the undesirable ones.

William still wanted him physically, and that was something. It was infinitely better to have the body of the man he loved, than have the heart of a man who refused him. Richard had needs too.

William rolled over and looked at him. "You're not asleep," he said in a hushed voice.

"Not yet."

"What are you thinking of?"

Should he tell him? William *had* asked. "I'm thinking of how lovely you are," he confessed.

"Really?"

"Yes."

The lad appeared delighted, even if he wasn't in love anymore. Richard wondered if he saw it as a validation. He had won. That was all right; Richard was used to losing.

"I'm thinking of how lovely your mouth and hands are," William whispered.

Richard chuckled quietly, unsurprised William chose to take the conversation in that direction. "Look at my hands," he said, holding them up. "Small and bony, nothing to speak of. I'll give you that they're skilled at lovemaking. Many a man seems to have enjoyed them."

"And your mouth too?"

"Yes, amongst other things."

They both giggled, and William shifted a little closer to him.

"Do you like my hands?" William asked.

Richard felt William's fingers lace between his own and clasp him tightly.

"I like all of you."

"You've not had all of me yet."

"I will."

William sighed lightly as he murmured, "I hope you do like me. Unlike you, I've no proof I'll be any good. You know you're the only man I've ever touched, ever kissed."

Perhaps that was part of Richard's interest in the lad. He might be mistaking possessiveness for love. That could not happen. It wouldn't be fair.

"You're young," he said wistfully, "there will be plenty of other men, believe me. I am but the first of many."

William snuggled a little closer to him. Richard felt William's hard cock press against his thigh through their hose.

"Take me tonight. I don't want to face danger without knowing what it felt like to have a man inside me."

Desire pierced Richard, and he stiffened, but he could not give in. He'd suffered enough bad luck already and had no need to court any more.

But he did need William. He was desperate to hold him and kiss him again, to feel the heat of the lad's bare skin pressed against his own. And he wanted more—to see William's face look up at him as the lad knelt at his feet, just before Richard enjoyed the warmth of his mouth and the skill, or charming lack thereof, of his tongue. He wanted to bury himself deep inside William's body and then give up his own arse in return.

William was right. They had no idea what they faced, though Richard didn't expect danger unless they were caught. He didn't want to regret refusing William, but he would regret it more if he lost him later.

Perhaps if the request were accompanied by words of love, he would have relented. It needn't have been true meant, just convincing enough that he could enjoy it. When William said it that first night,

Richard had been shocked, but now he longed to hear it again. Bennett had been correct when he said Richard snatched at affection. But why shouldn't he? He was just a man, and most seemed to crave it.

Richard didn't respond.

Eventually William continued. "Please. I know you can feel me. I need you. It will be hard all night and all day tomorrow, and it will distract me. Do you want me to die with this throbbing between my legs?"

Unable to help himself, Richard laughed. "No man ever died for wanting a lover. If you need a reason to stay alive, then I promise I will do so many things to you when we get back to London. I'll do new things, things that will make your eyes roll back and your head spin with pleasure. But you have to wait."

William let out a grunt of frustration and rolled away from him, onto his back. "How long will this take?" he muttered.

"A week. Two at most."

Another grunt. "I will have baubles as big as my head."

"Good. We will be able to exhibit you as an oddity when we arrive in Cambridge, and that will help us get into the college."

William didn't laugh. "Is it bad luck to make myself come off?" he asked seriously.

Richard's breath quickened. "I don't know."

"Now we will find out."

It took all Richard's effort and will not to pounce on William, but he could not stop himself from looking, though there was in truth little to see in the dark. William kept his hand beneath the blanket and didn't even glance at him, keeping his eyes shut the whole time. This wasn't a seduction, he just wanted satisfaction, and this was a glimpse into his most private world where he achieved it alone. Watching him was more arousing than if he had undressed before Richard and looked into his eyes.

The fire's orange glow lit William's face, showing intense concentration followed by absolute pleasure. As a smile spread across Richard's face, he wondered if he looked the same.

His own cock ached to be touched, but he let it be. If he was going to come off, he would have done it with William. He was too superstitious to risk the mission without the reward.

William left the bed to find a rag to clean himself. When he returned, he cuddled up to Richard and murmured good night. His breathing slowed and deepened a minute later when he fell asleep.

Richard kissed his nose gently and then allowed himself to doze off too.

Chapter Sixteen

Two days passed, and when they arrived in Cambridge late in the afternoon, William was tired from the walk. He had at least slept well the night before, although the bed was not as comfortable as their one in London. He could only hope he got such a good night's rest that evening as he expected the following day to be busy.

Richard got them a room at an inn, but they didn't do any more than stable the horse before they went out again, this time looking for one of Richard's acquaintances. Richard walked with purpose, but William found he could do no more than trudge along beside him, trying not to fall behind.

"Where are we going?" he asked wearily.

Richard was scanning his list of contacts and didn't look up as he replied, "We're going to meet a man I haven't seen in many years."

"Must we do it now? It is almost dark, and we have been traveling all day. Aren't you hungry?"

"I'm hungry and tired with it, but this is the best time to catch the man."

Richard tucked the papers away in his doublet. He didn't look hungry or tired, despite the long walk. If anything, he appeared invigorated. When their eyes met, William saw the same nervous energy in them that he himself had felt back at the bookshop and when he was on stage.

"Who is he?" he asked, as the excitement of the job returned to him.

"Roger Danbye. He is an important man in your new world. He recruits undergraduates to spy for him."

"Scholars are spies?"

"Some. It's much more civilized than anything I ever did, or most of the other spies I've worked with, for that matter. Danbye prides himself on that. He's Bennett's rival."

The goldsmith probably had plenty of those. "I like him already," William replied wryly.

Richard chuckled. "You don't have to like him. You're not going to meet him."

"You said I was to be involved."

"And you shall be, but you will make a terrible spy if you want everyone to know it."

He was right again, and William accepted the comment silently. "Am I to listen in?" he asked, focusing on the task at hand instead of his shortcomings.

"No need. I'll tell you everything I know when we are done. Just wait in the hallway. I want him to know I have an extra man for stage work if that is to be my way in. I don't want him to think you're a spy."

There was a certain thrill in hearing himself described that way—William Moodie, spy. He hadn't even known that people were employed to do such things until a few days ago, and now he was on his way to see one of the most important men in the country. Well, he was on his way to sit in his hallway.

"What will I be doing at the college?" he asked, hoping for something a bit more inspiring.

"I don't know yet. That depends on Danbye. I won't be revealing our mission to him, but he might still give me something useful if I can spin a good yarn. If he can get us in for his own benefit, then we can do Bennett's job at the same time."

So Richard did not expect Danbye to know anything about the list…. "Why would Bennett send you to his rival?"

"He didn't. He has provided me contacts, but I'll use none of them unless we're desperate. In fact, I would rather they don't know we're here. If Bennett does want you arrested, then any one of them could be looking for us. It would be better to rely on our wits than their help."

To William, that seemed sensible, but he wasn't sure his wits would have taken him to a man so similar to the one they were trying to escape. "Is this Danbye safe? If he is worse than Bennett, then this could be an even bigger mistake."

Richard looked at him seriously now, all cheer gone. "He knows Cambridge better than anyone and can open any door. If I'm careful, he might be the best help we can get."

"And if you're not?"

"I would prefer not to think about that."

They walked on in silence until Richard stopped across the road from a large redbrick house. It was close in size to Bennett's and could boast plenty of large windows, but that was where the similarity ended. It had no embellishments bar a few Tudor roses, no nods to the current architectural fashion.

"That is his home in the town," Richard whispered to William so no other would hear. "Danbye ought to be in by now. He has numerous jobs—justice of the peace, recruiter and master of spies, and he takes time for his own gentlemanly pursuits. He spends his evenings 'entertaining' undergraduates, although you couldn't call the gatherings lively. They all sit around talking about Catholics and Puritans and gossiping about the court, most of whom they have never met."

William thought Richard seemed to have a lot of details about a man he claimed was his lover's rival.

"How do you know all that?" he asked. "Did you spy on him?"

"I let him recruit me once after an argument with Bennett, and I soon learnt his habits. Needless to say, my employment didn't last."

"And you're sure you want to go to him now?"

"I don't want to. It's the best plan I've got."

That was the other thing that troubled William. "What exactly is the plan?"

"In the past, I usually arrived with the company, someone having suggested a performance. That is how Danbye would expect to see me, which is why he must be made aware of you. I want him to know I'm still in that world, but as there are only two of us here, I will have to offer my services another way. I need him to think I'm desperate to avoid Bennett, not that I'm working for him."

They approached the house together. Richard appeared nervous, while William acted casually bored. They both had parts to play, and William's was no problem. Sitting in the hall wasn't going to be terribly stimulating. He could only hope Richard was already in character.

Richard knocked on the door, and it was answered a minute later by one of the servants, who seemed surprised to see him.

"Master Brasyer!"

"How are you, good man?" Richard sounded friendly enough, but his face showed the strain.

"As best I can be. Come in, sir. I will fetch His Worship."

They entered the house and took seats in the gloomy entrance hall. The servant lit a lamp for them, but the space was large, and the wood-paneled walls provided little in the way of illumination.

William gazed into the darkness around him, feeling ill at ease. He did not show it, and he ignored Richard fidgeting beside him. He expected to be left alone while Richard was ushered into a room to see Danbye, but that did not happen. They waited together, the master given no more courtesy than his boy, until the justice eventually arrived in the hallway, carrying a larger lamp.

William knew him immediately as the head of the house, his fine dress and look of contempt at their appearance at his door proving it. Danbye was well into his fifties, heavyset, with hollow gray eyes that matched his ashen hair. Even in the dark, William could see the shadow of a beard on his face. He looked tired and unwell.

Ignoring William, he addressed Richard with resignation. "Brasyer? I assume you're not here for my society."

Richard stood and bowed deferentially. William copied.

"Your Worship," Richard greeted him. "Are you well?"

"Well enough to stop Goldfox from expanding, if that's what you're here about, though I'm not sure there's anything for him here. Undergraduates need more than full purses if you want them to work. Flattery is still the currency in these parts."

William may not have liked Bennett, but he got the impression he was better than Danbye at that. William kept his eyes turned to the floor but looked up when the justice asked, "Who's this boy?"

Danbye's tone was suspicious rather than interested the way Bennett had been.

Richard turned to introduce him. "My stage apprentice. He has come to learn the Fenland accent."

"From me?" Danbye snorted.

"I brought him only because I did not want to leave him alone at our lodgings. He is not a worldly youth."

"He can't have been your apprentice very long, then," Danbye muttered. "He'd better stay here."

William returned to his seat in the dark, and Richard was led away.

RICHARD FOLLOWED Danbye through the dimly lit house. He'd not stayed there long, but he remembered the dark rooms and the dour decor well. It had been something of a shock after living in Bennett's home.

He was taken to Danbye's study, which was well illuminated by a roaring fire. He was offered no seat and noted his host chose to remain standing too. This would be a short visit.

Danbye waited for him to speak. Richard knew he would have to choose his words carefully, though he felt he was at no risk from this man. He just didn't want to give away too much.

"Have you heard from Goldfox?" Richard never referred to him as Bennett with Danbye.

"Should I have?"

"I suppose not. I haven't spoken to him in some years, and I rarely meet mutual acquaintances. I just wondered how he was."

"I've no idea, and I am surprised you asked. I heard you'd fallen out again some years ago, but I assumed that wouldn't last."

Danbye didn't sound suspicious, but Richard knew from his words that he was.

"We're not friends now," he said with a tinge of sadness he did not need to fake. "Not that we ever were, in truth."

"I know what you were."

Richard met Danbye's eyes and saw judgment and disappointment in them. He wasn't their sort of man, but he hadn't revealed their secret. Danbye spent his time dealing with scholars and probably couldn't afford to publicly threaten their type.

"Yes," Richard murmured, "I was fiercely loyal to him once."

"And now?"

"I've long given up spying, and that is all he ever wanted from me."

"And yet you're here in my home." Danbye finally took a seat in a large, high-backed chair and stared at him pointedly. "I can't believe you came to me just to ask after Goldfox."

"I will talk plainly," Richard said, although he had no intention of doing so. "For two years my company has toured the provinces, and we now have little to our names. I came to Cambridge to see if I could acquire some information to sell."

"To Bennett?"

"If there is no other buyer. I can't afford to be proud, but I won't approach him until I have no other option. I decided to offer you my services first."

Danbye appeared to be thinking on the offer, but Richard was sure that whatever Danbye came up with would already be in his mind. They were just playing the game.

"I may have a job for you," Danbye said. "It is one I would prefer my own men do not do, and I know I can trust you with sensitive matters."

Richard had not told even Bennett Danbye's secrets. He'd made a promise never to speak on them, and he only nodded, solemn and silent.

"Have you brought your players?" Danbye asked.

"Just my apprentice. I couldn't afford the time or the cost of bringing the whole company. I need money quickly."

"A pity. They would have made things easier. But there are other ways."

Those "other ways" would be similar to Bennett's. Richard would do a few jobs if he must and use whatever Danbye gave him to get into Trinity. "What do you intend me to do?" he asked.

Danbye reassessed him one final time. Richard let him, confident he would find no fault.

Satisfied, Danbye said, "It's come to my attention that within one of the colleges, there is a list of names that are of interest to those looking to remove the Queen from the throne."

That sounded familiar and would certainly explain why Bennett had said nothing to its purpose. "Traitors?" Richard asked carefully.

"Perhaps. Or innocent men being set up."

Danbye was good at protecting himself, but Richard noticed him spinning a ring around his finger. The list made him nervous.

"Whose names are on it?"

"That doesn't concern you."

"I need to make sure I get the right paper."

Danbye left his seat and went to a table at the back of the room. He had various stacks of papers, but Richard noted that he plucked a piece straight from the top of one pile and didn't need to search for it. This was a pressing matter.

"You will know the list by the handwriting. It is kept by a man named Jacob Hobbes, hidden within his private room at Trinity College, but it was written by one of my men."

Richard took the paper and looked it over. It was a poem, and not a very good one at that, written to an older woman the writer was in love with.

"Apologies for the subject matter, but this is all I am able to give you," Danbye said. "You may dispose of it when you're done."

Richard folded the note and tucked it into his doublet. "Why can't your man do the work? Is he a traitor?"

Danbye shook his head solemnly. "Not at all. He was a good man who risked his life getting close to his killer for me. Now he's dead. Making that list was the last thing he ever did."

WILLIAM WAS growing cold in the hallway. He wrapped his arms around himself, tucking his hands into his armpits for warmth. Sitting down allowed his feet to swell, and he knew they would hurt when he stood to walk back to the inn. With no comfort to be had from Richard, it would be a long night.

He stared around at the darkness, knowing that anyone could be watching him. It was an unnerving thought, but he forced calm into himself and exhaled loudly, as if intensely bored by the whole business.

He hoped that, if someone was watching, they would be convinced. He was a bit bored in truth, as well as cold and tired. They probably would be too.

Closing his eyes and resting his head on the wall, he formed a plan. He let himself appear to be nodding off, then, with a start, shifted forward as if jolted awake at the last moment.

"Who is it? Who's there?" he demanded, prepared to relax back a moment later if no one came forward.

"Just me, sirrah," said the servant who had met them previously, stepping into the light.

William ignored the slight, though he was vexed. He wasn't used to being spoken to that way. "Does my master need me?" he asked.

"No. I've a notion to keep an eye on you, that's all. Your master kept bad company last time he was here, and I do not trust you to be any better."

Given Nick's previous behavior, William was not surprised. "His last apprentice let him down," he acknowledged, "but I am a man of good character."

"I don't know his previous apprentice, but I suspect he kept him up rather than let him down," the servant replied with a wink as he sat next to him.

William feigned ignorance and outrage on Richard's behalf. "What do you mean?" he gasped. "Are you slighting my master? Give me your name, you bastardly fellow. His Worship must hear how you speak of his guests."

The servant seemed amused by the display. "You may call me Jack, and I mean no harm. I liked Master Brasyer when he was here. He was generous and kind."

"Then explain your words."

"I mean exactly as I say. He kept bad company and had to leave because of it. You are more than welcome to complain about what I have said, if you wish to embarrass him. His Worship forgave him the indiscretion, but your master could not remain in his employ after that."

So Jack knew what Richard had done for a living. This man was a pair of eyes and ears, and William wished he'd not drawn him out. Better that Jack watched him in silence for an hour than he give something away now.

"That was generous," he said grudgingly.

"Master Brasyer was a good worker."

It had to be a test to see what William knew or how good he was at deception. He felt doubly stupid for inviting it.

"What did he do here?" he asked, affecting an obvious curiosity. "Did His Worship have an acting troupe? In truth, I have been told by many people to keep away from him, that he has a wicked past, but no one will give me any details."

It worked. Jack stood and said, "I know little. Only that he had undesirable friends."

At that moment, a door creaked open, and Jack scurried away, leaving William alone in the hallway.

He stood and dipped his head, waiting for Richard and Danbye, but the justice did not approach.

"Come," Richard said, "Let's get back to the inn."

They let themselves out and walked back in silence.

William was full of questions, but they would have to wait. Richard wasn't looking to see if they were followed, but William wasn't going to turn around and check. Eventually, they were back at the inn, carrying bowls of thick vegetable-and-bacon stew upstairs. Richard had a large loaf of bread to share between them tucked under his arm, and William couldn't wait to get into it.

"Can we speak now?" he asked when they entered the room. He hurried across to place his bowl on the table and then sat gratefully on a stool.

Richard joined him. He tore the bread in half and assessed the pieces to determine which was slightly larger. He gave that one to William. "We may talk."

"Well? What happened?"

Richard gave all his attention to the spoonful of hot stew he was blowing on. He didn't look up as he responded, "I negotiated a second pay for the same job. You will be a wealthy man."

"Me?"

"Apprentice on the stage or not, I will pay you handsomely for a job well done here. You will have real work to do."

William knew Richard was generous, but this was well beyond his expectations. There had to be a catch. "So Danbye knows about the list too?" he asked casually as he stirred his stew, waiting for it to cool down. "Is his name on it?"

"That is what we are to find out. Whoever sold him the information probably sold it to Bennett as well."

Richard still didn't look at him. Their eyes had not met since they left Danbye's home.

Abandoning the spoon, Richard dipped a small chunk of bread into his dinner, blowing on it when he raised it to his lips. William fought the urge to press for more details, making himself wait. He wanted to know if Richard would tell him unprompted.

Richard began to eat in silence, keeping his eye on the bowl. William didn't begin his meal, though he was hungry. He let Richard see he waited.

"You may ask if you wish," Richard said eventually, "but I will speak no more if you don't. As I said before, it will be safer for you not to know."

That might be true, but William wasn't only worried for himself. Richard knew everything. "Just tell me what expensive secret you're hiding. I'm not a fool. Your generosity can only be linked to my danger."

Richard put down his spoon and looked up at him. "Danbye said it's a list of traitors to the Crown."

William's heartbeat quickened, and he began to sweat, but he kept complete control of his outward appearance. He couldn't show Richard his weakness.

"We can't do this," he began. "If we are caught—"

"We will end up dead. I know. But if we don't do it, you will be hanged for thieving and I will be done for murder when I get hold of Bennett."

William would far rather take his chances as a thief on the run. "Traitors suffer worse," he muttered, thinking he did not wish to see what his bowels looked like. "Death is a mercy to them."

"I know. I won't force you to take part, but if you do, you will receive Danbye's payment, which will be a large enough sum to buy a share in the company when you have completed your training. This will either guarantee your future or destroy it."

"And if I refuse?"

"I will do the job alone. But you will have to leave the company. It would be too dangerous for you to remain with me, knowing what you do. Repercussions aren't always swift, and I'll not let you suffer for something you took no part in."

William had become too used to taking risks for Richard. He wouldn't let him do this alone. "I'll do it. I'm not leaving you. Not now."

For the first time since they left Danbye's house, Richard smiled. "Thank you." He took up his spoon and began to eat again.

William joined him, but his earlier mistake played on his mind. He should confess. "I think I gave myself away this evening. I guessed I was being watched, and I drew a servant from the shadows. I'm sorry."

He explained to Richard the full content of his conversation with Jack, and Richard was unperturbed.

"I wouldn't worry," Richard said. "I would be more concerned if you gave anything away about our reasons for being here. Bennett and Danbye are old rivals, but they're fighting the same battle. I've known them to work for each other's benefit in the past, each knowing the value of a favor owed. If Danbye thought arresting you might help Bennett in some way, then he would do it."

They finished their food, and Richard fetched the papers. Richard reread their instructions while William looked over the poem.

William couldn't help but laugh. "'Raven-haired mistress,'" he began, giggling to himself, "'keeper of secrets and my heart. In your eyes, I see only light. We come together in blackest night....' This doesn't even have rhythm, let alone beauty."

"I wrote it for you in earnest," Richard teased.

"I know you didn't because we have barely come together at all."

"Give me time." Richard winked. "It's an example of the handwriting on the list we are to find, that's all."

After a time, they swapped papers and William familiarized himself with the details of the job. He expected to be climbing into bed shortly afterward, but when he stood to leave the table, Richard shook his head.

"There's more?" William asked wearily, easing back onto his stool.

"Not much. We must discuss what we will do if we are caught."

It would be a short discussion. "I know exactly what I'll do. I'll tell everyone Bennett Goldfox is the biggest traitor in England. I'll tell them he moves against the Queen even as we speak, so she'd better hurry up and chop his head off."

"That is a tempting thought," Richard said without humor. "But I think the blame should be placed with Danbye. It would ensure you are better protected."

"If I've been caught with a list of traitors, I've got bigger problems than a charge of theft."

"That depends who we're caught by. We are nothing—the scum sent to do the job, not the men who'll benefit from it—and if Hobbes finds us, our loyalty should be negotiable. It's a slim chance, but you should prepare for it."

The dagger in his bag was William's only preparation for an encounter with Hobbes, and he intended to do nothing but threaten with it. All he knew of Danbye was that the man kept Richard's dalliances secret, and William thought he deserved a place in heaven for that.

"I won't blame an innocent man."

"We can if it's the only way to save you."

That was in the back of William's mind, of course, but he wasn't sure he wanted anyone, even a stranger, dying for him. "No. I wouldn't feel right."

Richard tidied up the papers and gave William a sympathetic look. "I understand how you feel, but from Danbye's point of view, this isn't about you, even if you are my only motivation. Do not spare him a thought. He has not scrupled about such things. You can't in this business. Why do you think I got out of it?"

"But you're not out of it, and one day that could be you being betrayed."

"That day has been and gone. You are nothing to Bennett, and look what he tried to do to you. I've seen Danbye do similar. Who would question the word of the local justice of the peace? I like him no better than Bennett. He was good to me once, but that's because I know his secrets. Don't think that's an indication of his character."

William was more concerned about his own, but he said nothing. He wouldn't lose sleep over Bennett, and if Richard said Danbye was no better, then that was good enough. It had to be.

Richard tucked the papers back into his bag and undressed. "Come," he said, "We've a busy day tomorrow. It's time for bed."

After two days' walk, William was tired. His feet were still sore, and he was glad to lie down. He was almost grateful Richard would not be interested in his body that night. But Richard didn't avert his eyes when William undressed, intense longing on his face.

Climbing onto the bed with him, William said, "You told me that was bad luck."

Richard gave him a devilish look that betrayed his lust. "I'm only looking at you," he said mock innocently. "That can't be too bad."

"You can't see your face."

Richard laughed and pulled William close to him. William wriggled in his grip and turned so Richard was at his back. He could feel Richard's excitement and found his own cock was swelling too.

"This must be bad luck," William said. "You are enjoying it far too much."

"You're right," Richard agreed, but he didn't let him go. "I'll not do any more than hold you now, but tomorrow all this will be over, and I may do to you whatever I like. One more night and I won't be holding back."

William tried not to imagine what that might be, knowing he would not sleep until he came off if he spent time thinking about it. Instead he let his mind linger on the comfort he got from Richard's embrace, the pleasure of knowing a man like Richard could want him, and most of all, the happiness he felt at his situation, no matter how bleak it had once appeared. Richard didn't just desire him, he cared about him too, and that thought sent William off to a contented sleep.

CHAPTER SEVENTEEN

DAWN WAS breaking, and William looked across at the college, with a frown on his brow. He wasn't an educated man, but back in Oxford he considered himself a local and had admired the colleges there on many an occasion. They were quite spectacular.

This one boasted some impressive parts, but much of it was a building site.

"That's Trinity?" he asked, wrinkling his nose. "I think the Oxford colleges are better."

Richard stood next to him, surveying the building for entry points. "I don't know," he said, eyeing the main entrance. "I think it'll look good when it's finished."

"I hope we're not staying that long, but I grant, if the gate is anything to go by, the rest will be remarkable."

"That's more like it," Richard said, rooting through his bag. He found a folded paper and checked it before handing it over. "You must tell them that when you ask for work."

"Work?"

"This is a letter of recommendation from Danbye. The story is that you have worked for him for two years and are now looking elsewhere for a contract."

William looked it over and noted that Danbye described him as a good worker, and honest, which was a kinder reference than he would likely ever receive again. "What do I do if they refuse me?"

"They won't. An understanding exists between Danbye and the Master of Trinity. He has several men claiming to be former employees of his working at the college. You'll be accepted without question and given the job of bedder."

"That sounds suspiciously like the same job everyone else thinks I've got," William said wryly. He could only hope he would not be expected to work the first day.

Richard grinned at him. "There is no bed work, not until we're done, anyway. You'll be like a servant, cleaning and tidying the scholars' rooms. Your job will be a simple one. You need only get into Jacob Hobbes's room and open the window, through which I will enter. After that, you must leave the grounds immediately and return to the inn."

Open a window? *That* was to be William's contribution to the job? Richard might as well do the whole thing himself. "That's it?" he scoffed. "You behaved as if I am to do something dangerous."

"It is dangerous. If you are caught helping me—"

"What is dangerous is you climbing through a window in broad daylight," William said, unimpressed with the plan. "Everyone will see you scrambling in, and that is if you are lucky. If he is on the upper floor, you won't be able to get in at all. If I can enter easily to open the window, then I can find the list too. No one will question why I am there going through his things if I am to be tidying them."

"A man died because he wrote that list," Richard muttered in reply. "Hobbes isn't likely to leave it lying around. This needs someone with experience, someone who knows where to look."

"Then why aren't you applying for the position? Is it beneath you to play a servant?"

Richard gave him a withering look. "I can play a servant, all right, but think how many people have already seen me do it. I played in Cambridge as often as I did Oxford in the last two years, and I am well-known to many of the scholars here. I wouldn't be surprised if the servants remember me too."

If only we had the costumes and paints.

William grinned, a new plan forming in his head. They had a razor, and he could surely find a suitable disguise somewhere within the college. They would just have to improvise.

AN HOUR later, he stood in the corner of the college's bustling kitchen with the steward, a tall, slim man with white hair that needed a cut and an expression that failed to hide his irritation at William's arrival. He'd probably been pressed into taking on a number of men he didn't want because they'd previously been employed by Danbye. William did not blame him for his mood.

"You worked for the justice?" the steward asked wearily, having done no more than glance over the letter and inspect the seal.

William shrunk back slightly, hoping to appease him by appearing unthreatening. "I did, sir," he murmured.

"Why did you leave?"

Realizing that he should have prepared a convincing lie, William simply said, "He's a good master, but I'd done two years. It was time I moved on."

The steward glanced at the letter again. "You're not a local, and he's given no mention of your background. Where are you from?"

Now William was on surer footing, glad of his heritage because it made the lie come easily. "I'm from Oxford, originally. I worked at Christ Church, and I first came to Cambridge to work in one of the colleges."

"Really? Well, we are affiliated to Christ Church College, so I can check that," the steward simpered. He looked like he would enjoy discovering one of Danbye's men was a liar.

William's heart sank. It would take the steward weeks to check with the college and he would be long gone by then, but if he'd been playing a longer game, he would have given himself away. It was a blow to his confidence, but it lasted only a moment. He was determined to do better.

The steward handed him over to another servant and disappeared off to more important work.

William was left with a woman who introduced herself as Eleanor. She was attractive—dark-haired with bright blue eyes, full lips, and clear skin. She appeared well proportioned, with ample breasts and skirts to match, and she was a good age, being maybe thirty.

"I'm William." He gave her his best smile.

"Lovely to meet you, William. You can help me today, and we will set you up with your own rooms tomorrow. Can you read?"

"Yes."

She looked as if she expected no less. "You're one of Danbye's men, aren't you." She made it a statement rather than a question. "I'll fetch you a list of students, and you can arrange to swap rooms with the others if you want to."

Why he would want to was left unsaid, but William realized Danbye's spy ring was not as secret as he hoped. The servants knew everything, and William wondered why Danbye didn't just pay the ones in situ to do the work. Perhaps they had their own loyalties already.

"Now," she continued, "some advice. These young masters can be trouble. You're a handsome young thing. Watch yourself with some of the students, and the scholars too."

William giggled. "You're telling me they would be more interested in me than a beautiful woman like you? I'm not sure whether or not that's lucky for me."

"I've got my admirers." Eleanor chuckled, her eyes dancing merrily. "But you would be surprised at the types we get here."

"I've never heard anything like it," William teased.

They left the kitchen, and Eleanor gave him a short tour of the building. William noted the exits, hoping he'd worked out correctly which door Richard would be standing behind. He didn't want to open the wrong one and find himself somewhere he ought not to be seen.

Soon they were walking to the private rooms, and William didn't have long if he wanted to charm her into leaving him alone on his first day. He had vague ideas of asking to have a go at cleaning by himself so she might inspect the work afterward, but, as ever, he wasn't sure of the details.

"So, tell me about your admirers," he said casually as they approached the halls.

When she met his eyes, he made sure he wore a cheeky grin.

"Not much to tell," she replied, giving him a wink. "Some were better than others."

"Tell me about the good ones." She hesitated, so he asked, "How am I supposed to impress you if I don't know how your other suitors did?"

"You're far too young to be trying to impress me." She laughed. "But I do like a verse."

"Poetry? I don't know many poems." That was no lie. Most of William's reading had been the Bible and the odd chapbook he'd borrowed. He knew verses that were passed around the fire at night, but none suitable for wooing women. Then he remembered the terrible ode he'd seen the previous evening. Hoping she might be charmed by its lack of skill, he said, "Raven-haired mistress. In your eyes, I see only light."

It did not have the desired effect. Eleanor became pale and whispered, "Who are you? What are you doing here?" She stumbled into a wall, trying to get away from him.

Just his luck to find *the* raven-haired mistress among every woman in Cambridge. "What?" he asked, hoping he appeared confused and concerned. "I don't understand? Have I said something I should not?"

She relaxed a little physically, but her manner told William she was still wary of him. "Where did you hear that poem?" she hissed. "How could you know it?"

"I used to work for the justice of the peace, Roger Danbye, just as you were told. I saw the poem on the table in his library and read it one day while I was cleaning. I thought it was good."

He did not think it worth the ink and paper, but if she was the subject, it might soften her again. Then he allowed a little suspicion into his voice as he asked, "How do you come to know a poem that His Worship keeps? I've never seen you there during the day."

She blushed heavily. "I have never been to Danbye's home during day or night, don't you worry about that. I heard it from the lips of the man who wrote it. He was a student here."

"Oh, that makes sense," William said, dismissing the subject as if it no longer interested him. "The master seemed to know so many students. If you like it, then you should get him to write it down for you."

"Too late for that," she murmured, her fear being replaced by sadness. She put a protective hand over her belly and said, "He's gone, and he won't be coming back."

William didn't press for details, having a fair idea what fate had befallen her lover and half an idea what had befallen her. "You know," he said quietly as they began to walk again, "Danbye doesn't care for that poem at all. I could get it for you."

She stopped abruptly and then carried on, staring straight ahead. "How?"

"I'd borrow it and then lend it to you. If I forget to get it back from you, well, that's my fault. He won't miss it. It's in a pile of scrap paper… well, I assume it still is. He may have used the back of it for a note by now. If you let me sneak away, I can have it back here to you in an hour, but you must do a favor for me first."

Now she looked at him. "How do I know you're telling the truth?"

He could hear the hope in her voice. She sounded like she would risk a lot for that poem.

It was a fair question, and William wasn't sure how to put her mind at ease. Eleanor had revealed she knew enough about Danbye's men to know he wasn't what he appeared, but that hadn't worried her when it came to her former lover. Deciding a degree of honesty would win him more trust than another lie, William said, "You have nothing but my word, but I promise I speak from the heart. I will get you that poem if it buys me the smallest assistance. I'm not here to lie to you or trick you. Do you think Danbye would waste his resources on that?"

They reached the end of the corridor and were about to enter the hall of residence where they would begin their work. Eleanor paused at the door, holding it shut. William waited while she decided his fate, watching her weigh up the risk in her mind. It was just a piece of paper, and as time went on, William began to worry he hadn't offered enough.

Then she asked, "What would you have me do?"

"Nothing that will compromise you," he promised, disguising his relief with a gentle tone. "I just want directions to a fellow's room."

"Who?"

"Jacob Hobbes."

Eleanor balked, and there was fear again in her lovely blue eyes, but William let her have her dignity and did not try to comfort her. After a moment, she bit her lip and controlled it. "May I ask what interest you have in that gentleman?"

"I have none personally, but I have been asked to pay special attention when cleaning his room."

She didn't question by whom, but she did whisper, "You're too young to cross him on Danbye's behalf. You will not get the best of him. He is a dangerous man."

"I can protect myself," William replied, thinking of Geoffrey's dagger, which he'd tucked into the back of his hose again that morning.

"He won't fight you fairly. No weapons, no fists."

Having already suffered a taste of how unfair these men could be, William didn't want another false accusation against him. Thankfully he knew he wouldn't be around long enough for that.

"I am not afraid, and you needn't be either. Just tell me the room number. That's no secret, and I will find it out easily enough without your help. You're doing no wrong."

"You will get me the poem?"

"I promise."

She hesitated only a moment more before whispering, "He's in number twenty-three. He's lecturing now and will be seeing students at dinner. He will be here all afternoon, so make sure you clean the room this morning."

William beamed at her. "Thank you. I promise you won't regret this. I will fetch your poem and meet you outside the kitchen just before noon."

Silently she handed him the keys to the corridor then left him to his work.

William hurried through the door and along to number twenty-three. He gave a brief knock and then let himself into the room.

It was a large, bright space, well ordered but with a lot packed inside. Everything William owned fit into his bag, but this man had stacks of papers on his table, plus a drafting table with yet more papers and instruments, and William counted twelve books on a shelf along the wall. There were also a number of curiosities: animal bones, unusual shells, hideous masks, and terrifying dolls. It was a horrible collection, and as William eyed the simple single pallet bed in the corner, he wondered how Hobbes slept surrounded by it all.

He hoped to find robes and a cap, but there were none hanging. He left the room, locking it behind him, and was thankful to find them two doors down.

A few minutes later, William stepped outside to a long garden where Richard waited, crouched among the bushes. No one else was about, and seeing him, Richard jumped up from his hiding place and hurried to the door.

Richard appeared relieved to see him and was in high spirits. He had a boyish charm without his beard, and William quite liked his new look.

"You took your time," Richard teased. "I was sure I would take root before you arrived."

William swatted his arm in jest, finding Richard's happiness infectious. It was all happening now, and soon the job would be done. They had a lot to be pleased about.

"I've got you a scholar's robes, Hobbes's plans for the day and the key to his room," he mock chided. "You could greet me better than that."

He handed Richard the disguise, and his master was clearly thrilled with his work.

"You clever thing," Richard said. "I'm sorry I doubted you."

"That's not even the best of it. We have almost an hour to search his room."

"If we're still here in an hour, I will weep."

Richard donned the robes and held out a hand to indicate William should lead the way.

"There is just one thing," William said, remembering his promise. "Have you got the poem on you?"

"Yes, but let's keep it safe until we are inside."

"Good idea. I've promised it to a woman who helped me."

Richard's good mood disappeared in an instant. Stone-faced, he asked, "You told her our plan?"

"I told her nothing but that I worked for Danbye previously, just as we agreed, and that he has the poem. She knew her lover was connected to the justice in some way or another, and she appeared to believe me. Right now she thinks I have sneaked out to steal it for her."

Richard frowned, but his face showed concentration rather than anger. "Is she the raven-haired mistress?"

"Who else would want it? I think even less of it now I've seen her. She's far prettier than the poem."

Richard raised an eyebrow at that comment, and William heard a tinge of jealousy in his voice as he said, "I've seen a new side to you these last few days. Not just this nymph. You called the hostess in Cheshunt 'sport,' which is fun in itself, but there's little sweeter than winning the match. Have you a liking for the fairer sex? I'd encourage you to have a taste if you do. Your life will be a lot easier if she pleases you."

Richard meant well, but William's life would be no different, no matter how stiff a girl could make him. William's cock liked many men, but he was only besotted with one. Surely that was the same for any man, no matter where they took their pleasure.

William let him worry just for a moment before he dropped his voice and murmured, "You needn't worry about that. Unlike your last apprentice, you'll never taste a girl on my lips."

He turned to take them back through the door, but Richard caught his arm.

"You were there, weren't you, in the barn?"

"Close enough. I was outside it. Spying."

"What else would my lover be doing?" Richard murmured. "Sometimes I think you were put here by God just for me."

William's stomach fluttered the way it had when he first saw Richard on stage. Richard gazed at him with a tenderness William wasn't used to. For the first time, he wondered if Richard Brasyer—handsome, wonderful, perfect Richard Brasyer—had fallen in love with him.

The look lasted only seconds before Richard was hurrying him out of the garden as if nothing had passed between them. William had to accept that this was not the time nor the place to speak on it further.

Richard walked four paces behind him. When they stepped inside, William fought the urge to turn and look at his master, but focused instead on the job at hand. That wasn't hard; now Richard was in the college and it was all coming together, William was beginning to enjoy himself.

The same excitement he'd experienced at the bookshop overtook him. He felt brave and clever, and more than anything—despite everything that had happened to him—he felt he had luck on his side.

Soon he was back at Hobbes's door. He knocked and then let himself inside, glancing around to make sure he was alone. He went straight to the papers on the table, looking up when Richard entered a moment later.

"Excellent. Get to work on the room. If someone finds you in here, it needs to look like you've been doing something. You're new, so you can claim you thought I was Hobbes if we are found in here together."

William busied himself dusting the collection of oddities. They were filthy, and he guessed the other servants wouldn't touch them because they were frightened. It didn't appear Hobbes picked them up often either.

While William cleaned, Richard searched around for a box or small chest but found nothing hidden away. Next he shuffled through the papers on the table, not bothering to replace them neatly, and muttering obscenities under his breath. This was not part of the plan.

William went to the table and rearranged the papers Richard had displaced. "For someone who is supposed to work in secret, you're very careless," he said, keeping his tone light, though he was worried.

"You're supposed to be tidying the room, remember? Neaten it," Richard muttered.

William decided to say what they were both thinking. "Maybe it's not here. If it's that important, then maybe he keeps it on him all the time."

Ignoring the suggestion, Richard said, "Help me look if you won't clean up."

Glancing about, William lit upon the books on the shelf. They were as dusty as everything else, and it was obvious they didn't see much use either. Some had beautiful covers, while others were plainly bound. Drawn to the decorative ones, he opened a few to their front pages so he could see what they were about.

"Richard, stop a moment," he said eagerly. "Look at these books. Alchemy, astrology, magic...."

"Of course he has books. He's a scholar," Richard muttered, shuffling through yet more leaves of paper.

"Sounds more like a witch to me, but I think this stuff is just for show. He doesn't appear to use any of it."

William didn't believe in witchcraft, having seen a kindly spinster accused for no more reason than a need to blame someone when a series of misfortunes fell upon the village. She knew herb lore, which seemed to make people suspicious when they didn't have a headache, a toothache, or a feverish child.

Picking up the only clean book, which was on magic, he glanced inside but found it was in a language he didn't understand. It had been annotated in English, however.

"Look, he's marked this page," he said. "'A spell to bring misfortune.' That's vague."

Richard did not respond, so William turned a few more pages and found a folded piece of paper. "There's something hidden in here," he said, pulling it out and handing it to Richard, whose attention he now had in full.

Richard snatched it up and opened the paper, then took the poem out of his bag to check whether it was done in the same hand. He looked it over silently and appeared confused.

"Is that it?" William asked.

"I think so." Richard handed William the poem, not taking his eyes from the list. "Danbye's man wrote this, all right, but I've no idea what it's for. It's certainly not a list of traitors. It's titled 'The Unlucky Ones.'" Richard's eyes scanned down farther, and then he screwed up his face as he muttered, "He's not on here. Bennett's name isn't on the list."

"Then what are we doing here?"

"I've no idea."

William grabbed a quill, ink, and paper. "Here, write down the names."

Richard could write fast, and William was impressed with his speed, having never written more than his own name before. It was legible too, and William noted names he knew to be members of the Queen's court, among those he did not. Then he saw Richard copy down *Roger Danbye*.

"Danbye? That doesn't bode well for my wages."

"The Queen herself is on this," Richard replied, not bothering to look up at him. "These aren't traitors, but some of them are powerful people."

"Are you sure we have the right paper?"

"Look at the hand. This is the one. Danbye told me he knew little; only that these names were of interest to those who wished harm to the Queen. This could be a list of their greatest enemies for all we know."

William tucked the poem into his jacket and finished tidying the room while Richard completed the list.

A few minutes later, they were at the door, about to step into the corridor. William poked his head outside to check the hall and saw a man dressed in college robes walking toward the room.

He quickly stuck his head back inside and whispered, "Hide, someone is coming! I'll tell you when he's gone."

William stepped into the hallway again and found himself staring straight at the stranger. He was a young man, maybe only a year or two older than William, and was clearly not one of the students. He removed his cap to reveal hair so blond it was almost white, which was made even more striking by his light gray eyes. His coloring put him far from William's usual type, and William wouldn't have called him conventionally handsome, but something about the man was disarmingly attractive.

"Who are you?" the scholar asked. "I've not seen you before."

The question was simply put, with no hint of anything more than polite interest, but William could tell from the way the fellow's eyes moved over him that he was being appraised and admired quite openly. This was what Eleanor meant when she told him to be careful.

William lowered his head a little. "I'm the new bedder, sir."

"What's your name?"

"William."

Reaching around him, the man, who he now realized to be Jacob Hobbes, turned the handle and opened the door. "Come on, then, William," he said. "Let's see your work."

William prayed to a God he didn't believe in that Richard was well hidden. As he stepped inside, head down still, Hobbes muttered, "You left the window open."

"My mistake," William said. "Please forgive me, sir."

Hobbes closed the window and walked back toward him. William tensed and didn't bring his eyes up to meet the scholar's, hoping Hobbes took it as respect for his rank rather than William's nerves.

He waited for Hobbes to speak but instead felt the scholar's hand touch his head gently.

"You have lovely hair," he said, stroking it.

William looked up at him now, wondering if he would have to buy himself out of the room.

"Thank you, sir," he said apprehensively. Then he felt a sharp pain as a strand of hair was yanked from his head. "Ouch!"

Hobbes chuckled and took the hair over to his table, where he laid it down against a piece of parchment and looked at it intently.

William waited, showing more patience than he felt, while Hobbes inspected the hair. His initial impression faded entirely, and now he found Hobbes only disconcerting.

"Are you a virgin?" Hobbes asked, not looking up at him.

"Pardon?"

Hobbes glanced across at him, a smile playing on his lips. "It's a simple enough question, isn't it?" he asked casually. "Are you innocent? Pure? Are you a virgin?"

William blushed. "I'm not, no," he muttered. He might not have felt Richard move inside him yet, but he wasn't untouched.

"Pity." Hobbes took up the hair and tossed it into the fire.

"May I leave now, sir?"

"Go. Go on."

William moved quickly. His hand was on the door when Hobbes said, "Wait!"

William held his breath. He turned slowly to see the scholar warming his hands by the fire.

"Air the sheets tomorrow."

"Yes, sir," William said and let himself out before Hobbes could issue any more orders.

As the door shut, William paused and let out a long-held breath. He could hear Hobbes laughing heartily and was pleased to be out of his company. He walked down the corridor but set a fast pace, eager to escape now the work was done. It would be better to get away now than when someone noticed a set of robes missing, but William had made Eleanor a promise, and he intended to keep it.

Besides, the farther he got from the room, the better he felt. The excitement was returning, knowing he was but a few minutes from being outside and on the way to Danbye's home, where payment awaited. Richard had promised William he would be rich, and he was thrilled at the prospect. If he was careful with the money and invested it wisely, he could be set for life.

But even better was the promise of what would come that evening. They would soon be on the road to London, and luck would no longer be required. He would be in Richard's arms that night.

He arrived at the meeting point to find Eleanor already there waiting for him. She appeared nervous and looked around to make sure nobody was paying them too much attention as servants passed.

Ushering him into a storeroom full of buckets and rags, she whispered, "Have you got it?"

William removed the paper and handed it to her. "Here. Your poem."

Carefully she unfolded it and looked it over. Tears pricked her eyes, and she rested her hand on her belly again. "Thank you," she whispered as she tucked the paper away against her breast.

"Was it about you?"

"He said it was. But he said a lot of things. I should have known better than to trust him."

Taking her hand, William said, "I think you do him a disservice. He surely must have loved you if he wrote you that."

She smiled as she wiped away her tears. "Yes, I suppose so."

William let go of her hand and gave her a hug instead. "I have to go now," he told her gently. "I won't be back. Thank you for helping me today."

She bit her lip awkwardly and whispered, "It's only fair I tell you that Danbye's men told me they don't know you and you've never worked at the house. They're waiting for you outside the kitchen door, and I don't think they intend to talk about it."

Realizing the poem had brought him a lot more than the number of Hobbes's room, William was grateful for her honesty. "I swear to you, today I am Danbye's man. You believe me, don't you?"

"I don't know what to believe, but you seem decent and have kept a promise, which is more than most others he has sent to work here. Come with me. I'll show you another way out."

She took him to the students' entrance, which they had passed on the tour. A guard stood beside it. William saw Richard exiting ahead of him, still in disguise. Richard went past without being questioned and walked on toward their horse.

Eleanor led William to the door and loudly said, "Go on, hurry through and back to your master. Next time woo your girl on Sunday, in your own time, so you won't need to come through here. I shan't help you again. You'll have to go through the kitchen and be late."

He hurried past the guard, who paid him no mind, and stepped onto the street. Richard, still dressed in his scholar's disguise, was readying the horse.

This was it, William thought, it was over, and they would be back on the road to London within the hour.

"Run, William!" Eleanor shouted.

He didn't look back as he took off, but he could hear men behind him, bellowing to the guard to help stop him.

"I have a sword!" Richard shouted, turning around and throwing off his disguise. He drew his weapon and ran toward them, sword in one hand, dagger in the other.

William chanced a look over his shoulder; his pursuers were nervous now Richard had come to his aid.

"I've Geoffrey's dagger," he told Richard and pulled it from the back of his hose. It was still sheathed, but he turned and brandished it at the men regardless.

"Get to the horse," Richard barked.

Richard protected him, and William ran to the horse and clambered up onto the animal's back. He was surprised to find the hunter wasn't spooked, but any horse of Bennett's had probably been in similar situations before.

"Let's go!" he shouted to Richard, who lunged once more at Danbye's men, pushing them back.

Richard turned and dashed over to William, who helped pull him onto the horse. They were gone moments later, galloping up the road and around the corner.

"Where are we going?" William asked.

"Danbye's house."

"Will it be safe there? Those were his men."

"I know. They recognized me even without my beard. That's why they let me hold them back with the sword instead of rushing me. One of them definitely knows me. At least, he has known me. He was in my bed more than once when I worked for Danbye. I don't think he'll reveal who I am."

They stopped at the inn first, collected their things, and made two more copies of the list before paying for the room. Richard left extra to ensure that anyone asking would find they'd not stayed there. Then they were on their way to Danbye's home, and this time when they arrived, William was allowed into his private study.

Danbye sat at a table, reading through some papers. He looked up when they were ushered in but didn't greet them.

"Is it done?" he asked, addressing Richard and ignoring William.

"Your name is on the list."

The justice's face grew pale. "Good Lord." He put a hand to his chest as if he was in pain.

Richard went to him, pulling one of the copies he'd made out of his doublet. "It's all right. You needn't worry. It's not a list of traitors, unless the Queen is one herself. I made you a copy of it."

Danbye snatched it out of Richard's hands and looked it over, his face taking on a similar frown to the one Richard had sported when he first saw it. "The Unlucky Ones," he muttered. "The first four men named are dead."

Richard made no comment, and they waited silently until Danbye put it down on his table and looked out the window.

"Your Worship," Richard said gently, "there is the matter of my payment."

Danbye looked at him irritably. "Of course." He took a purse from his belt and handed it to Richard. "Twenty-five sovereigns. Please count them. I have been distracted this morning, and I may have missed one."

Richard did so, and the money move from the purse to the table and back again. It was all there, and if Richard meant what he said, it was all William's. More money than he had ever possessed in his entire life, and though he knew he should save it, a little might be spent on new clothes, a dagger of his own, and perhaps some sent to his mother and father so they could see how well he'd done.

AN HOUR later, William was buying late lunches for them at a tavern on the road back to London and feeling like a king.

"You're still my apprentice, you know," Richard said, eyeing the slabs of roasted meat on their table. "I don't want you wasting your money on me."

"I'm the best-paid apprentice in England. I can afford to treat you."

"Don't get used to the cash. You will never have it again. You may need it to run if the watch is still after you. If Bennett withdraws his complaint, then you must use it instead to secure your future in the company. Don't touch even a farthing, and when your apprenticeship is finished, you can buy yourself in."

"I will," William promised, but he wasn't listening. All he could think of was getting a private room upstairs and spending the whole afternoon sitting on Richard's cock. He doubted his lover would allow that either. Nightfall seemed a long way away, but there were other nice things to talk about while they were on the road.

The innkeeper approached their table and asked if they'd picked up any news on their travels. William knew little, but Richard had a wealth of it from his time spent touring and as the weather was turning to rain, he obliged the man.

William sat and listened in silence, chuckling when he noticed them doing so, but not paying attention. His mind kept returning to the garden, where Richard had made the comment that William was just for him. It wasn't the first sweet thing Richard had said unprompted, but it was the first time he hadn't pushed William away afterward. That must mean something.

Last week, the idea of Richard being in love with him went straight to his groin, but this was different. Now what he felt warmed him all over, instead of the heat pooling in his lap the way it always had before.

The passion remained and would not be dampened, but there was so much more between them now. Richard brought him comfort and contentment mixed with a little of the old hope. Richard had always been talented and handsome, but now William could testify without a doubt that he was brave, generous, and caring too. He finally knew Richard, and he was truly falling in love.

But he couldn't tell Richard, not right now. Two days had passed since he'd told his master he did not love him, and even after the look they'd shared in the college garden, he would be embarrassed to recant. Richard had said he liked William's childish declarations of love, but William felt the immaturity behind them too keenly. Now he would hold back, wait until he was sure Richard would admit he felt the same. It would be all the sweeter knowing that when he confessed his feelings, they would be returned.

And there was no question they wouldn't be. William felt very satisfied as he ate, confident that, like everything else since he left home, he would get what he wanted in the end.

CHAPTER EIGHTEEN

RICHARD ARRIVED at Bennett's home at midday. The return journey had been slower, and they'd trudged through driving rain for five days, leading the horse slowly through thick mud in many places where the roads weren't well maintained by the locals. Worse still, the inns were busier and there were no private rooms to be had. Every night they slept on boards shared by as many as six men, and they hadn't a moment to relax as they wished. Richard's mood would have been low even if he was not about to confront, for the last time, a man he despised.

A servant he didn't know let him inside and left him in the hallway. A few minutes later, Bennett greeted him alone, carrying a pile of dry clothes and towels.

"Richard," Bennett said warmly, "this is a happy surprise. I wasn't sure you would be back."

"You knew I would return. You left me no choice," he growled, glancing toward Bennett. He didn't dignify him with eye contact.

Bennett looked around. "Is William hiding somewhere?" he asked. "That's sensible."

Richard made no comment. He wasn't going to give anything away until he had Bennett's word he would not harm the lad.

Bennett waited for him to speak, nodding when he accepted he would not. "Come. I believe I owe you some money."

They made their way to the bedchamber. Inside, Richard went immediately to warm himself by the fire, Bennett following in his wake.

"Dry yourself and put these on," Bennett said. "I'll find something for you to take to William, wherever he is. I'm sure he is as cold and wet as you are."

Richard silently took the towel and carelessly threw the clothes on the floor. He could see they were new, probably even made especially for him, knowing Bennett, but he was bothered only by the fact they were dry. He wouldn't be bought with an expensive doublet and hose.

He shrugged off his leather cloak and began to undress, aware of Bennett bringing a chair toward the fire for him to drape his wet clothes on, but he still refused to look at him. There were times in the past when he'd arrived angry, desperately wanting an excuse to forgive Bennett. This was not one of them.

Bennett took some older clothes from a trunk and packed them into a bag for William. Then he sat on the edge of the bed and watched as Richard dried himself.

"Must you look at me?" Richard asked, feeling his naked skin burn beneath the gaze. He focused on toweling his body, working as quickly as possible so he might get his hose on.

Bennett shrugged. "This may be the last time I see you. Forgive me if I try to take as much from you as I can."

"You'll get nothing but contempt," Richard muttered. He would have made something of those words once, and the truth of it shamed him. How could he ever have loved such a man? He tossed aside the towel and picked up the new hose, then pulled them on hurriedly.

Bennett sighed, and Richard looked at him again. The genial mask was gone, and his face was expressionless. Richard wondered if he knew how to show any other emotion. He imagined that everything at the inn had been no more than a well-rehearsed act.

"What if I give you something you want?" Bennett asked. "I can guarantee you William's safety immediately."

"You must guarantee his safety permanently." Richard stalked toward the bed and leaned over Bennett. Richard was half-dressed, wearing his hose and no shirt, but he didn't care anymore if Bennett looked at him through lustful eyes. In that moment, he cared only for William's well-being. "No more false accusations," he continued, "and no knives in the dark. I will destroy you if he is ever harmed, even if you seem to have no connection to it. You should pray he has a long, healthy, happy life, because it will be on your head if he doesn't."

Bennett dragged his gaze away from Richard's body and looked up at him. "He will suffer no ill from me. I have no wish to hurt you through him. As for now, I made no charge against him when the watch arrived, and I explained the error was on my part."

Richard was used to lies from Bennett, but he believed him this time. Taking the matter further would have been inconvenient if he truly planned for William to work. If the lad had no value, things might have been different.

"Good," he muttered, then returned to the clothes and continued to dress.

"No thank-you?" Bennett asked.

It was no jest, but Richard couldn't stop himself from letting out a bitter laugh. "Thank you? For endangering him? No, you'll have no thanks from me for that."

"I never intended to see it through."

"I know perfectly well your intent. You want him to work for you. I'll wager you still think you'll get him to spy on me."

"The boy might as well have the extra money. If he won't do it, then I'll find someone else. I like to know that you're well."

"And I like my privacy. Why can't you leave me alone?"

Bennett gave no response. Richard had expected him to make another play for his good favor, especially after his words of love at the Spurre, but Bennett was silent.

"I knew you didn't mean it," Richard muttered. His face burned again at the shame of knowing that once he would have clung to the memory of that meaningless confession.

Bennett left the bed and went to fetch Richard's money from the hidden chest. Unable to look at him, Bennett mumbled, "It was the desperate act of a man who knew he'd lost the only thing he had that was worth anything. Pay it no mind."

He removed the panel and then paused to take a deep breath. Richard could see the mask going back on again. It had to be exhausting playing the part of Bennett Goldfox all day.

Changing the subject to something more comfortable for them both, Bennett said, "I will have your funds in a moment. What have you for me?"

Richard riffled in his bag for a copy of the list. "I found Hobbes and your list, but it wasn't what I was expecting. William dealt with him and said Hobbes behaved strangely. He is of our type, quite young, and appears to have a superficial interest in the occult."

Bennett hummed agreement. "I have managed to learn a little of his character. He is apparently fascinated by the study of magic and astrology, though I am assured not the practice. I believe alchemy is more his specialty."

"We saw no evidence of that, save from some dusty books and curios. Whatever he's up to, I don't believe it to be sorcery."

"Did you make me a copy of the list?"

"Yes. You weren't on it."

Bennett's face clouded. "You can't have seen the right paper, because my name is definitely on it. You will have to go back."

"I've made no mistake. We turned his room over and only found one that it could be. I was able to procure more information from Danbye, and he provided me a sample of writing in the same hand."

"Does his name appear?"

"Yes."

"I knew it," Bennett muttered. "Stupid man."

"This is not a list of traitors."

"That is for the Queen to decide."

Given her position on the list, Richard would wager every man and woman on it was innocent of treason if nothing else. But Bennett didn't know that, and Richard thought him a little too quick to sell out Danbye. "I think you'd better explain," he said, "because I'll not be caught in a battle between you and Danbye. I went to Cambridge to save your life, not incriminate your rival."

"This is no battle. Danbye told me I was in danger. He said there was a list of what he believed to be men to be accused of treason, in Hobbes's room at Trinity."

"So you decide to reward your old friend by accusing him instead?"

"I cannot ignore a threat of treason, not in my position. If there were another way—"

"Spare me more lies, Bennett," Richard snapped. "I know how low you can sink. You would sell even me out to protect your position."

Bennett narrowed his eyes, and breathed deeper. Although he kept his cool, he was furious. "He invited it by using us to go searching for his damned list. He must have wanted you to do the job because he didn't trust his own men."

"Then he is a fool, because he could have trusted them a hundred times over you."

Silently Bennett left the chest of coins and took a small box from beneath the bed. Richard had seen it before and knew it housed all Bennett's most important correspondence. He'd never looked inside it. Bennett unlocked it with a key he kept around his neck, and from the top removed a small scroll that carried Danbye's seal.

"Here," Bennett said angrily, "read what it says. Your name was supposed to be on that list too. I assure you he meant no one else when he referred to 'those closest to me.'"

There was a knock at the door, and Bennett stalked over to it, shoving the letter into Richard's hand as he went. "What is it?" he roared as he opened the door.

"Apologies, master," a terrified servant in the doorway said, "but the entertainers are here."

Bennett composed himself and grunted that he would deal with them. He left the room, leaving the door open and Richard alone with Danbye's letter.

A quick glance told Richard all he needed to know. This time, at least, Bennett did not lie.

He went to the box to replace the letter and recognized his own handwriting on the one that had been below it. Addressed to Nick's mother, it was the letter Richard had written for his former apprentice, not knowing that he wrote of his own progress. Bennett had said he kept it, but Richard had not believed him.

Curious, he picked up the letter below and found another in his hand, this one addressed to Bennett. It was nothing, just a curt note to say he'd made Nick his apprentice. He was surprised Bennett had kept it. Below that was more general correspondence between them, of no particular interest, and then farther down, he found his love letters, written during the few short periods of happiness they'd shared before it all went wrong again.

After adding a copy of the list of Unlucky Ones, he put the box away. When he turned around, he found Bennett leaning in the doorway, watching him.

"I am expecting guests," Bennett said calmly. His hunched shoulders revealed he was still tense, but he was controlled. "You are more than welcome to stay. I would like you to stay. I don't want you to go."

"I have to get back to William," Richard replied quietly. "Your horse is stabled at the Swan Inn. I've left a copy of Hobbes's list with everything else written by my hand."

Silently Bennett nodded and returned to the chest. Richard busied himself, gathering his wet clothes into a bundle and putting on his cloak, but he watched Bennett while he did so.

Bennett picked up a small sack he'd discarded when he went to get the letter. He grabbed fistfuls of coins from the chest and stuffed them into the bag. Richard watched it stretch under the weight of them.

"Here," Bennett said eventually, when he could fit no more in. "This is your payment. It's a little more than we arranged, but if I am not to see you for a while, then I will feel better knowing you are provided for. You can come back if you need to."

Richard took the heavy purse. It was hard to lift, and he knew he would need William's help to carry it back to the inn. The thought of the young man grounded him, and he realized just how much he'd changed since William came into his life.

"I will not be back," he said, picking up the bag of dry clothes Bennett provided for William. "I can't protect you anymore. William is my priority now."

Bennett bit his lip. "Are you sure about him?" His voice was throaty, but he did not choke on the words. "Are you in love with him?"

"Yes."

"And your feelings for me?"

They were gone. Bennett was too late. "How long could I love you when you gave me nothing in return?"

Bennett nodded a mournful acceptance and stared into the fire. "It is not easy for me to speak of such things. My position does not allow me the luxury of emotion. Still, I hoped I'd done enough. You have the ring, and all the meaning attached to it."

Richard had not forgotten it. "Your mother's wedding ring," he murmured as he slipped it from his finger.

"Left to me for whomever I intended to marry. I gave it to you."

"I should go," Richard said, hoisting the purse up and into his bag. "I need to get back to William and tell him this is over."

Bennett didn't take his eyes from the flames. "I wish you both well. Good-bye, my love."

Richard left the room, clasping the ring in his hand. As he approached the front door, he saw a servant he knew, who went to open it for him.

"Thank you." Richard stepped out into the rain. Then, before the door could close behind him, he held out the ring. "Please give this to your master and convey my sincerest apologies that I am unable to keep it."

RICHARD FOUND William a quarter of a mile up the road, drinking ale and eating bread and cheese in the Swan. Not wanting to enter with such a heavy purse in his possession, Richard gave the stable boy a penny to fetch him outside. It had been an effort to carry it, and he'd staggered up the road with the bag in his arms, fearing the strap would break if he forced it to take the weight.

A few minutes later, William entered the stable carrying the food and drink. They both sat on a long, thin bench that stood against the wall, and William offered some food to Richard, who gratefully shared it with him.

"Is it over?" William sounded nervous for the first time in several days.

"For good, I hope, but I make no promises when it comes to Bennett."

Tension leaving him, William slumped back against the stable wall. "Good. I'm so tired I haven't the energy to run again."

"I'm sorry to disappoint, but we've a heavy load to carry back." Richard opened his bag to reveal the large purse.

William's eyes widened and a grin spread across his face. "I can manage that."

An hour later they arrived back at the Spurre. Given their desperate flight the previous week, Richard expected questions from the inn's regulars and a few of the locals, but only the young street seller paid them any mind, and William soon saw him off with a promise to see him in the bar that evening.

Neither of them returned with any expectation of getting their old room back, but Geoffrey had persuaded the innkeeper to save it for them and keep a good fire going. Richard hoped Geoffrey paid for it out of the money he'd left him and not from the purse he'd been gifted.

The rest of the company were away performing, so Richard and William entered alone and dropped down onto stools by the fire to remove their boots and wet clothes. Soon they were naked, letting their skin warm up and their hair dry in the heat of the blaze.

Richard stole a glance and saw William watched him in return. He had a look of nervous anticipation on his face, and his cock was half-hard.

"That was a long journey," William said. "It's nice to be back in our room, with our bed. I think I will sleep well tonight."

"Are you tired?"

"I was exhausted coming up the stairs. But now I'm looking at you, I'm not so sure."

Richard held out his hand, inviting William to come to him. The lad straddled his lap and kissed him hungrily while Richard explored his body with his hands. First he touched his nipples, sensitive little nubs that with a bit of friction grew as hard as his cock. Then he trailed his fingers down William's sides and back toward his pert, round buttocks. Richard squeezed the cheeks and gently pulled them apart to expose the entrance to William's body.

Withdrawing a hand, he brought it up to his mouth and wet his finger before offering it to William, who did the same. William did not try to kiss him again and looked down into his eyes. Richard returned the hand to his arse and brought the spit-slicked finger to the hole. He rubbed lightly but didn't push inside.

"Tease," William whispered and shivered as he clung to Richard, leaning forward so he could push himself back toward the finger.

Richard toyed with the pucker, felt it contract and relax as the lad's excitement grew. He withdrew his hand, then picked William up and carried him to the bed. After laying him down gently, Richard climbed on top and kissed him, letting him feel the full weight of a man's body pressing down on his own.

Richard pulled away to kiss William's neck, shoulders, and then down to the sensitive nipples again. He licked and nibbled until William begged, "Please go lower. This is wonderful torture, but I want more. I want you inside me."

It might be fun to play with William and make him wait, but Richard wanted only to please him now. He moved lower, swiftly dragging his tongue down beyond William's thick cock, glistening with his juice, past the tight balls, and down to his arsehole.

"You must talk to me," he said. "Tell me if it hurts. It might be quite a shock the first time something goes in."

Biting his lip, William replied, "Your finger will not be the first."

"You told me you were a virgin," Richard murmured, not that he minded if William was not.

"I am, but there's more than one way to know your own hand."

Fresh desire shot through Richard. "You are sinful," he whispered, a wicked smile playing on his lips.

William blushed slightly. "I have spent so much time longing for you. I had to have something."

"You thought of me?"

Now William grinned. "Most of the time," he teased.

Richard returned to his work. He had much to live up to now. He dipped down between the cheeks and lapped at the hole. William responded with low moans and pulled his legs farther up and apart, allowing Richard to worm his tongue a little deeper, which drew a fresh gasp of pleasure from him.

"Have in me," William begged. "I can't wait much longer. I am desperate to touch myself."

"You need oiling."

Richard withdrew to fetch a small bottle from his bag. When he returned, he took his time slicking his fingers while William watched impatiently, and his face told only of frustration with the time he took. Richard did not wish to make him beg again.

Slowly, gently, Richard pushed a finger inside his lover. William took it with ease and shuddered in ecstasy when Richard found his most special place. He moved his finger slowly at first but found it didn't take much work to stretch William's arse. The lad had trained himself well, but Richard knew he would still have to be gentle with him as William took his first cock.

When it was finally time, Richard pushed in carefully, letting him get used to the unknown length and girth. He'd used a lot of oil, most of the bottle in fact, but still he was cautious. Richard had been hard a long time and wanted nothing more than to pound the lad's arse as deep and as fast as he could, but he held back and waited, making William's satisfaction his own.

Progress was slow, inching inside him. William's face strained, but his prick was as hard as ever, and when Richard pushed to the root and stopped, his breathless young lover said, "You must kiss me now. Do it like you really mean it. That is how I have always imagined this would be."

So Richard did. He lay down on top of him again and kissed him deeply, with a force he'd not allowed himself before. He let himself dominate, capturing William's mouth and pressing it into submission, stealing the lad's breath. When William moaned, Richard pulled back just far enough that he could look down at him, letting the tips of their noses touch while their lips could not. William looked up at him, shivered, and closed his eyes, pulling Richard close again. The weight of him pushed his cock deeper still, and William groaned into his mouth as they kissed, angling his arse up to take in as much as he could.

At last William was ready, and Richard could move his hips. He lifted his weight up onto his hands so William might touch himself, and began a slow thrust, building speed as time passed and his lover grew louder. Then he felt the tight, hot squeeze of William's passage as he reached his climax, and they were both coming off together.

Richard was exhausted, but he wasn't quite done, not yet. He withdrew slowly, lay down next to William, and pulled him into his arms, pressing his lips to the lad's for one more long, slow kiss. He didn't want it to end.

But it must. William pulled his face away from the kiss but remained in his embrace and rested his head on Richard's chest, just as he had done when Richard first began to fall in love with him.

William was glowing. Richard felt glorious as William told him, "That was the best thing that has ever happened to me. I wish I could spend the rest of my life here in this bed. You are everything I hoped you would be."

"I wasn't bad, I suppose," Richard admitted modestly with a chuckle, "but don't think I've peaked. I've so much more to do with you. Perhaps you'll love me yet."

William's shy smile was back as he said, "If you keep doing things like that, I will."

"I'd better keep it up, then."

"Please do."

William looked at him expectantly, and Richard waited for more too, but neither spoke.

Leaving the bed, William continued, "And please don't tease me about love again. I'm ashamed of the way I behaved when we met." He wet a rag in the ewer and wiped himself down.

Richard pushed down his disappointment at the words and concentrated on the invitation. William had affection for him, maybe even love, and he might be able to admit it one day when his newfound pride mattered less. Richard could wait, and until that day came, he had plenty to comfort him.

"I won't tease you, I promise, and I would hate for you to suppress your feelings, be they good, bad, or indifferent toward me. You need never be ashamed of anything that comes from your heart."

"When we first met, it came more from my loins than my breast, and my head could not tell the difference," William confessed with an embarrassed laugh.

Richard smirked at that. "No need to explain. I have felt similar, in my youth. And for now, I have your body, which is just as worth having. You might surprise me again one day, if your heart catches up."

William bit his lip and returned to the bed. He sat next to where Richard lay and looked down at him, deep into his eyes, with an intense, searching gaze. "What of your heart now?"

"My heart?" William owned it, but Richard didn't want to reveal himself if his lover would not. "I am not ashamed of anything I feel for you. But I ought to be as careful as you are."

"Is that what we are doing? Being careful."

"I think it is."

William chuckled again. "You know, that is not my usual way."

"I had noticed."

"So I may as well tell you that, over the last few days, I have come to realize what it truly means to be in love."

That sounded pretty careful to Richard. As nice as it felt, he'd longed all his life to hear the words plainly spoken. "And?" he asked, a wide smile on his face.

"And I have fallen in love with you, Richard Brasyer."

Richard stared at him for a long time. He had believed he would never live to hear anyone he loved offer those words. He pulled William down and kissed him again, but the lad pushed him away.

"Well?" William demanded. "Will you not say it back to me? I told you I won't put up with any more teasing."

"Of course I love you." Richard laughed as William scrambled back into the bed merrily and kissed him.

Richard had nothing left, but he could feel William's prick already beginning to harden again. "Slow down," he murmured. "We have the whole of our lives for that. I'll see you all right in a few hours."

William cuddled up to him. "What now, then?"

What now, indeed?

Richard pulled him closer, and with a contented sigh, said, "Now, we rest."

VANESSA MULBERRY has been reading and writing since she learned to read and write. She has been an MM romance reader for a decade now and took up writing the genre because she loves happy endings and, ahem, happy endings. Her hobbies include Gin and Tonic.

She lives in Buckinghamshire (which is significantly less posh than it sounds) with her long-suffering husband and their adorable daughter.

You can find out more about Vanessa at:

Website: www.vanessamulberry.com
Twitter: @VanessaMulberry

A Night at the
Ariston Baths

MICHAEL MURPHY

www.dreamspinnerpress.com

OCEAN OF
SECRETS

JERRY SACHER

www.dreamspinnerpress.com

www.ingramcontent.com/pod-product-compliance
Lightning Source LLC
Chambersburg PA
CBHW060049260626
47160CB00005B/1632